THE

GATEKEEPER'S

PROMISE

D1484522

Eva Pohler

Published by Green Press

This book is a work of fiction. The characters, happenings, and dialogue came from the author's imagination and are not real.

THE GATEKEEPER'S PROMISE: GATEKEEPER'S SAGA, BOOK SIX Copyright 2014 by Eva Pohler.

FIRST EDITION

Book Cover Design by Keri Knutson of Alchemy Book Covers and Design

Library of Congress Cataloging-in-Publication has been applied for

ISBN-13: 978-0989999052
ISBN-10: 098999905X

Other Books by Eva Pohler

The Gatekeeper's Sons: The Gatekeeper's Saga, Book One

The Gatekeeper's Challenge: The Gatekeeper's Saga, Book Two

The Gatekeeper's Daughter: The Gatekeeper's Saga, Book Three

The Gatekeeper's House: The Gatekeeper's Saga, Book Four

The Gatekeeper's Secret: The Gatekeeper's Saga, Book Five

The Gatekeeper's Bride: A Prequel to The Gatekeeper's Saga

Hypnos: A Gatekeeper's Spin-Off, Book One

Hunting Prometheus: A Gatekeeper's Spin-Off, Book Two

Storming Olympus: A Gatekeeper's Spin-Off, Book Three

Charon's Quest: A Gatekeeper's Saga Novel

Vampire Addiction: The Vampires of Athens, Book One

Vampire Ascension: The Vampires of Athens, Book Two

Vampire Affliction: The Vampires of Athens, Book Three

The Purgatorium: The Purgatorium, Book One

Gray's Domain: The Purgatorium, Book Two

The Calibans: The Purgatorium, Book Three

The Mystery Box: A Soccer Mom's Nightmare

The Mystery Tomb: An Archaeologist's Nightmare

The Mystery Man: A College Student's Nightmare

Secrets of the Greek Revival: Mystery House #3

The Case of the Abandoned Warehouse: Mystery House #2

French Quarter Clues: Mystery House #3

Chapter One: A Short Honeymoon

The shifting hues of the Aurora Borealis danced above Therese as she lay with Than on a blanket on the frosty summit of Mount Thor—home of the world's greatest vertical drop. For their honeymoon, Than had brought her to Baffin Island in Northern Canada near the North Pole. The light show lasted several minutes until Helios appeared, bright and early at two in the morning. His golden cup would remain visible for a good twenty hours, which was precisely the reason Than had brought Therese to this spot.

She kissed the side of his face. "Spectacular," she whispered.

"I thought you'd like it." He pulled her more closely into him as the rays from Helios enveloped them in the sunrise. "It's the brightest place on Earth, next to Mount Olympus."

And the opposite of the Underworld in every way. Why did he still think she didn't love the house of Hades? Not wanting to hurt his feelings, she thanked him again and snuggled closer to him.

He yawned lazily. She rarely saw him so peaceful-looking.

They'd ridden polar bears, sang with narwhals, swam with baby penguins, and sunbathed with walruses. Than had thought of everything she'd enjoy. Therese felt like the luckiest person in the world.

Now it was cuddle time beneath the fantastic northern lights, which were fading in Helios's beams.

A movement near her ribs made her flinch. The babies were waking up.

"He's up high today," she said of the boy twin inside her.

"How do you know it's Hermes and not Hestia?"

"I sense them." She lifted his hand toward her swollen belly. "Maybe you can sense them, too."

He laid his large hand, with its thick, long fingers, up against her skin and waited. His eyes suddenly widened with surprise.

"Hestia! I can't explain how I know it's her!" His face beamed.

And he'd never looked sexier.

"Pretty amazing, huh?" She winked.

"She put her tiny baby hand up to mine," he said, astounded.

"They aren't like regular mortal babies, are they," she said without inflection. "They're so advanced."

"They *are* demigods."

"I can't wait to hold them in my arms."

He frowned.

"I'm sorry." She clapped her hand to her forehead. "I'm so stupid." She kept forgetting how he must feel, knowing he would endanger the lives of their children if he was in their presence once they were born.

"We should have a plan." The muscle near his jaw flexed.

She sat up and leaned over him. "We'll ask Hip to switch with you, just until the twins become adults—eighteen years tops. That's nothing to him, right?"

"It's a lot to ask."

"You could offer to give him breaks every day."

Than gave her a half smile. "But I'd still never see the twins awake."

"You could hold them in your arms as they slept."

"Maybe he'd do it—switch with me."

"I think he would. He loves you so much. So stop worrying, okay?" She leaned down and kissed him.

She could sense in the way he kissed her back that he was worried. Hermes and Hestia may never have the chance to get to know their father.

"A-hem," came an unexpected voice nearby.

The newlyweds turned their heads to find Dionysus, in nothing but a loin cloth, standing over them.

"Sorry to interrupt," he said. "But the Maenads are waiting."

***

Than was surprised to find that Dionysus had led them to Crete, near the palace ruins of Knossos.

"What's going on?" Therese asked.

"The Maenads have grown fond of the Minotaur and his labyrinth," Dionysus said.

Ariadne appeared with a scowl. "How many times must I ask you to call him by his Greek name? Is that so difficult?"

Dionysus turned to see his estranged wife glaring at him. "My apologies. Old habits."

"Make new ones," Ariadne said. Then she took Therese by the hands and asked, "How are you holding up?"

Than knew Therese was trying to be brave for him, as always. This was harder on her than it was on him.

Asterion emerged from the labyrinth followed by three Maenads and two Curetes.

"What, Curetes, too?" Than asked of the dancing men and their crashing cymbals.

"They heard the Maenads and came down from the mountain," Dionysus explained.

"They were just leaving," Asterion added. "Go on, men. Now's not a good time."

The Curetes skipped away in a rush of clangs and hops.

"I don't like this," Ariadne said to Dionysus. "I told you I didn't want this here."

4

"Asterion's never been happier," the god of the vine objected. "You said so yourself."

"The company has been good for him, but my nerves can't handle what the Maenads are about to do."

Dionysus wrapped his arms around her waist. "If we're to be together…"

"It doesn't matter," Than interrupted. "Let's just get it over with. The sooner the better."

***

Jen stopped outside the master bedroom door, her heart aching at the sound of her mother's sobs. She couldn't take the sorrow anymore. Jen had to tell her.

She tapped on the door and went in. "Mom?"

Her mother lay on her bed, hugging her pillow. Her whole body shook, but she stopped as soon as she heard Jen come in.

"Oh, hi there, sweet baby girl. Don't mind me." She wiped her swollen eyes with the bed sheet. "I'm such a mess."

"That's alright, Mom." Jen sat on the edge of the bed with one leg curled underneath her. "Maybe if you just got out more. It's too bad Mr. Stern hasn't come around in a while."

More tears poured from Mrs. Holt's eyes. "I just haven't been in any kind of shape for company lately."

"You haven't come out to help with the horses for three days."

5

"I'm not feeling well, baby doll."

"Remember when Dumbo died?"

"'Course I do." She wiped her face with the sheet. "Why do you ask?"

"You made Therese come help with the horses the very next day."

"I wouldn't say I *made* her."

Jen picked at the bed covers. "You pressured her enough."

"Now, listen here, baby girl." Her mother's face turned red. "You can't compare the loss of Dumbo to your brother. And I *was* out there the very next day. We all were. I'm just not well right now."

"Mom, I'm just saying…" What *was* she trying to say? Everything seemed to be coming out all wrong. "Never mind. There's something I want to tell you. Now don't freak out."

Her mother sat up on the bed, alarmed. "Oh, no. What?"

"It's not bad. It's good. Just promise not to freak out."

"How can I promise that if I don't know what it is?"

"You know how Pete used to say Daddy's ghost talked to him?"

"Pete was sick. He couldn't help it."

"We saw Daddy's ghost that one time, too. The night he died. Remember when we were all in your tub 'cause you thought a tornado was coming? Therese convinced us it was a dream."

6

"Now wait a minute…" Her mother pulled the covers back and moved to the edge of the bed.

"Just listen. This is gonna sound crazy." Jen was scared to death she was doing the wrong thing. Her mother would probably think Jen was sick, like Pete. But Jen couldn't take another day of her mother's pain. "I've been to the other side. Don't freak out."

Her mother looked exasperated. "What are you talking about, baby doll?"

"It wasn't a dream, either." Jen stood up and walked around to the side of the bed to get closer to her mom. "I went to the other side, and I saw Pete."

***

Hip made his way down the deepest path of the Underworld, determined to ask Pete's advice. The seer was already condemned, so what harm could come from using his gifts? Hip's heart was hurting, and maybe Pete could tell him what to do.

Wouldn't it be just Hip's luck that the moment he knew he was one hundred percent in love, it would be with a mortal, and it would be just at the moment the lord of the gods decreed there would be no more apotheosis? If humans couldn't become gods, how would he and Jen get their happily ever after?

Before he reached the iron gate of Tartarus, he sensed Pete and Tizzie down in the seers' pit, among the asphodel where the Phlegethon did not flow. Tizzie's wolf lay at her feet. Hip was still several yards from them, and Tizzie and Pete did not seem aware of Hip's presence.

"How can I not warn them?" Pete asked in a strained, almost tortured voice.

"The visions of seers aren't guaranteed," Tizzie replied.

"You don't believe in me."

"That's not it, love. Come here."

Tizzie's dark, slender arms wrapped around Pete's transparent neck, but fell through. She struggled with the illusion of embracing him. Her long, dark, serpentine curls lay limp without their usual animation.

Tizzie sensed him then and said in an annoyed tone, "Can we help you, Hip?"

"Let's ask him what to do," Pete said.

Hip opened the gate, scratching the iron against the rock, and then closed it behind him. He made his way past the flames of the Phlegethon, turned the dark corner, and went down, down into the deep pit of the seers.

"Hey, sis," Hip said in the most nonchalant voice he could muster. "What's up?"

"Everything," she said without humor. "This *is* the Underworld."

"Double entendre?" Hip asked playfully. "I mean, everything *is* up above us, and the Underworld *is* a hopping place, am I right?"

"If you're a frog," Pete replied.

"Ha, ha, ha. Good one." Hip snapped both thumbs in the direction of the seer.

"So tell us why you're here," Tizzie demanded, and her wolf gave one sharp bark.

"Well, I was hoping for some advice, but it sounds like *you* want the same thing from *me*."

Pete said yes at the same time Tizzie said no. The two lovers glared at one another.

"Whoa," Hip said. "I didn't mean to start a war."

"It's about the twins," Pete said. "Therese's twins."

"What about them?" Therese asked from around the corner as she escorted Than into Tartarus.

Therese had obviously taken Than's duties as the god of death. Than didn't look so hot. It was August, which meant the Maenads.

"You okay, bro'?" Hip put a hand on Than's transparent shoulder.

"Huh?" Than gave him a blank look.

"Give him a minute," Therese said. She put her arms around her husband. "Than, Baby? Do you know who you are?"

"Speaking of babies," Pete said. "There's something..."

Tizzie cupped Pete's face in her hands, and blood dripped from her eyes. Her serpentine curls lifted up in a hiss before falling limp again. "Don't."

"What's this about?" Hip asked. "I get that it's about the twins, but what about them?"

"Do you mean *our* twins?" Than snapped to attention.

"They can't live here," Pete blurted out. "Hades neglected to tell you *that* part of the prophecy."

Therese's brows bent together and her mouth fell open. "What are you saying?"

"The twins have to grow up among mortals if they're to fulfill their destiny," Pete replied.

As Therese and Than sought one another's eyes, Hip wondered what this would mean. Would Therese leave his brother behind and return to the Upperworld to raise their children?

Chapter Two: Confrontations

Thanatos was not one for sitting idle. It wasn't in his nature. Rarely, since the moment he had come of age and the duties of death had been bestowed upon him by his father, had he had a moment's rest. Even as he had been honeymooning with his bride, he had been working.

Now he wasn't sure which was worse, enduring the horrific pain of having his limbs ripped from him, or sitting in Tartarus waiting for his body to heal. Although Therese visited him each day, she had her duties and responsibilities, along with his, and couldn't stay with him for more than a few hours at a time. Unlike him, she wasn't adept at disintegration and found it hard to relax while doing a million other things. That left Than bored out of his mind and burdened with thoughts of his family's future.

Therese and the babies would have to leave him. It was the only way.

If he'd been in his body as he imagined his life without them, he would have cried.

So, as the days wore on in Tartarus at their unusually slow pace, Than distracted himself as much as he could. At the top of his list was a confrontation with Melinoe. He'd been putting it off, but now he had no more excuses not to speak with her.

He floated past the area of punishment, where Alecto was busy purging some evil soul of its wrongdoing, his screams as loud as they would have been using his human body. Unused to this part of the Underworld, Than shuddered and moved on, down into another part of the pit where the souls who never leave dwell.

Unlike the seers' pit, the deepest parts of Hades were alight with the flowing Phlegethon spiraling down in an almost vertical drop. The souls of the damned clung to the cavern walls. Most of them were silent in their misery, but others moaned or sobbed—usually the newly condemned who had not yet accepted their lot. At the very bottom of this pit were the Titans who'd been imprisoned by the Olympians after the great rebellion.

No one went down that deep anymore.

At last Than found the Malevolent sitting idly on a rock tossing pebbles into the river of fire.

She narrowed her transparent eyes—one black and the other white—when he approached. "What do you want?"

"Peace," he said, as he took a seat across from her.

"Peace is boring." She tossed another pebble into the fire.

"And this isn't?"

She floated up so that she could look down her finger at him. "Look, you have a purpose. You don't know what it's like."

"You could have one, too."

"I *had* one." She folded her arms and turned her back to him.

"Stealing souls and tormenting mortals?" he asked, but not without kindness. If he wanted her to cooperate, he didn't want to make her angrier than she already was.

She whipped around to face him again. "Your other sisters torment mortals."

That was the first time in centuries she'd acknowledged they were related. He looked at her for a moment, taking it in.

"What?" she said impatiently.

"Do you realize you've never called yourself my sister?"

She turned away from him again. "Quit changing the subject."

"Well, you must see the difference between tormenting evildoers to purge them of sin and scaring the hell out of innocent people."

She laughed and faced him. "One's a hell of a lot more fun."

He didn't have to ask which one she meant. "If it didn't mean robbing those souls of eternal peace…"

"Like what you're doing with these people down here?"

"These people made their choices."

"Well, which is it, Thanatos? First, you say I should have the opportunity for redemption because my father turned me into the monster I've become." She moved closer. "And now, you're saying that people are responsible for their choices."

He looked at her misshapen face—half white and half black. "You're different."

"Are you so sure? Look around you. Most of the souls down here never had a chance."

Than didn't know what to say. He stood up. "Therese swore an oath to spend eternity down here with you if any god in the Alliance treated you unjustly."

Melinoe flew back to her seat and sat down. "I should have known that was the only reason you came. Get away from me."

"Melinoe..."

"Get away from me!!!"

He planted his transparent feet firmly on the path and said, "I don't have all the answers, but if Therese has taught me one thing, it's that change *is* possible. But you have to want it too, sister."

Reluctantly he turned and flew back to the upper part of Tartarus.

He spent the next couple of days spying on Hip, who, he noticed, was not acting like himself. Hip's usual charm and quick wit had been replaced with dullness and despondency. Maybe Hip had become depressed over some news about Than's twins.

So Than beckoned to Hip one day.

"Come see me in Tartarus," Than prayed. "I'd like a word."

Hip appeared instantly. "You called, bro?"

"Yeah. Sit down."

Hip sat cross-legged on a nearby boulder. "If this is about the fate of your twins, I know nothing more than you."

Than sighed. "You swear, on the River Styx?"

"I swear."

Than slumped on a rock across from Hip. "Then what's on your mind. You've been moping around like a teenage girl who's just got her period."

Hip arched a brow. "That's a rather pleasant comparison."

"And apt. Wouldn't you agree?"

Hip shrugged. "Life sucks for me now, bro'. I used to have it good, see? I used to play all day and night without a care."

"What's changed?"

"You know the answer to that." Hip lifted his palms in the air. "Sometimes I wish we never would have met Therese. Things were better before."

"Maybe for you."

"I'm glad you got your girl, but it kills me that I'll never have mine."

"Why can't you? At least for the rest of *her* life?"

Hip cocked his head to one side. "Would you be able to live happily if Therese died a mortal?"

"No, but I'd take that over no life with her at all."

Hip stood up and turned his back to Than, facing the dancing flames of the Phlegethon. "Maybe. The only time we have together is when she sleeps. It's hard not to have her here with me."

Than stood and clapped a hand on his brother's shoulder. "I know what you mean. Therese and I are in the same boat."

Hip spun around to face his twin. "What are you saying?"

"You heard Pete. She'll have to go back to Colorado. Maybe she'll live with her aunt and uncle and visit me at night, I guess. I don't see any other answer, do you?" Than looked into his brother's eyes, hoping for an idea.

But Hip slowly shook his head. "Sorry, man."

As Hip was about to leave Tartarus, Hermes appeared.

"Lord Zeus requests your presence, cousin," Hermes said.

Than and Hip exchanged looks.

"It's Hip this time," Hermes said. "You holding up okay, Thanatos?"

"As well as can be expected." Than gave the messenger god a smile. "It's good to see you back in business. I can't thank you enough for what you did."

"Oh, stop," Hermes insisted. "I'd say naming your son for me is thanks enough and more than I deserve."

"You promised to come play night Frisbee over on Crete," Than added.

"And I will. Call me next time."

"Sorry to interrupt this sweet family reunion," Hip said. "But what could Lord Zeus possibly want with me?"

"Well, now. That's for Zeus to know and for you to find out." Hermes winked and turned again to Than. "Don't be a stranger." Hermes disappeared.

"Catch you later, bro," Hip said just before he followed Hermes to Mount Olympus.

    ***

As soon as Hip entered the court where the sun always shined, his mother crossed the room and embraced him.

"I'm so bored up here, and my mother is suffocating me," she whispered in his ear.

At that moment, Hip wanted to say, "I know how you feel," but he resisted the urge as he peeled his mother's arms from his neck.

From over his mother's shoulder, he met Aphrodite's smile. The goddess of love waved at him. Hip smiled back.

The Graces, sitting near Aphrodite, batted their eyes at him—all but Pasithea, whose face turned red as she looked away.

"Please tell me you've come to visit me," Persephone said. "And you're not here on business."

Hip squeezed his mother's hands. "I should visit, shouldn't I? I'm sorry I haven't. Shame on me."

17

Hephaestus waved from the door of his forge. Hip gave the older god a friendly nod.

Persephone smiled. "Well, you're here now."

Hip lowered his head and then met his mother's hopeful face. "Zeus called for me."

Persephone's smile faded.

"But I'll come by and chat right after I see him."

"Good."

Hip left his mother and crossed the room to the double throne at the back, where Zeus and Hera sat conversing with one another. He always admired the golden ruby-eyed eagle and three golden finches that adorned their throne. The two gods leaned close together, their noses almost touching. Hera's long red hair was loosed from its usual knot. Hip thought she looked more beautiful, less severe, with her hair down.

Ares, the twins, Athena, and Poseidon were not at court. Hip remembered Athena and her mother, Metis, had gone on a trip around the world together—making up for lost time, he supposed. Hestia was discussing something with Hecate and Demeter, who had thrown her arm around her daughter's shoulders the moment she had returned from Hip's side. Hermes played a light tune on his pipe while Cybele—or Rhea, as they had come to call her again—clapped her manly hands to the rhythm beside him. Despite the presence of this handful of gods, Mount Olympus felt abandoned.

The god of sleep waited patiently to be acknowledged.

"Aha," Zeus said. "Good to see you, Hypnos."

"Likewise," Hip replied. "You asked for me?"

"No one likes a dull boy," Zeus said. "The mortals are suffering. What pains you?"

Hip hadn't expected this direct question from the lord of the gods. His mouth dropped open, and he stared dumbly back at Zeus.

"It's the mortal girl, isn't it?" Hera asked.

"Of course it is," Rhea said.

"I knew it," Zeus said before Hip could reply. "Hermes, bring Cupid to me."

Hip glanced at his cousin, who looked up with surprise from his pipe. "Cupid? Of course, Father."

Hermes left the room.

Aphrodite flew over to Hip. "Father, what has my son to do with Hip's situation, if you don't mind the question?"

Rhea moved closer to Hera and crossed her manly arms.

Zeus got to his feet. "Sleep is very important to peace on earth, my dear—not that I ever expect to have such a thing, especially with Ares running around, making his mischief. As of late, mortals have been suffering from lack of good sleep. They are restless because Hypnos is restless."

"Lord Zeus," Hip began, feeling suddenly light and happy. Might Zeus make an exception of his rule against apotheosis for the sake of world peace? "Is this what I think it is?"

"And what is that, my boy?" Zeus asked.

"Do you mean to make Jen Holt like us?"

Zeus burst out in laughter. Hera even chuckled beside him, but Rhea frowned.

Hip's cheeks burned red, first with embarrassment and then with anger.

Zeus's face also turned to anger. "Make Jen Holt a god? You can't be serious, Hypnos! Don't you recall the stalemate that took place, right here in this room, just a few weeks ago? I had your brother with my lightning bolt at his throat. Poseidon directed his trident at Ares. Your father threatened to unhand me as he hid beneath his helm! In response to the demands of the Alliance, I gave equal footing to my sisters and mother in exchange for my own demand! Don't you recall what it was?"

"No more gods," Hip said glumly.

"Precisely!" Zeus bellowed. "So why should I change my mind so soon on the heels of that agreement? Nay, *oath*! We all swore an *oath*!" His face looked like an angry red bull about to charge.

Hermes and Cupid appeared beside Zeus.

But Zeus continued. "It was my one and only demand in a stand-off with my brethren! And you think I would dismiss it so easily? So soon? Because you are *sad*?"

"My apologies, Lord Zeus," Hip managed to mutter, his hopes dashed and his ego humiliated. "I will try to do better for the sakes of the mortals. Am I excused?"

"Not quite," Zeus replied, the red draining from his face. "Not quite, my boy. Aphrodite, bring me Pasithea."

Aphrodite turned on her heels and returned holding the hand of Pasithea, who looked nervous standing before the lord of the gods.

"What is this about, Father?" Aphrodite asked.

Hip held his breath as sweat broke out on his brow.

"Be careful, Zeus," Rhea warned. "Think this through."

"Hypnos, gaze upon your old fiancé," Zeus commanded, ignoring his mother. "Cupid, shoot him with your arrow."

Hip fell to his knees as the room began to spin. The thought of losing his love for Jen sickened him. He wanted to vomit. "Do not do this, Zeus. I beg of you. I will go back to my merry ways. You have my word."

He sensed Pasithea break into tears. He hadn't meant to hurt her. Surely she could understand. He turned back to see her face, and at that moment, the arrow struck him fully in the heart.

***

Therese was overjoyed when she re-integrated—a sure sign Than's soul had returned from Tartarus, rejoined his body, and resumed his godly status. She stood up from her favorite spot in the bat cave and smiled down at Clifford, as well as Cubie and Galin, who had been allowed to remain in the Underworld to keep Clifford company while their mistress was away on Mount Olympus.

Therese lifted her chin. "Than?"

He immediately appeared before her. The glow of his body brought more light to the cave.

She threw her arms around his neck. "I've missed you."

He laughed. "You've spoken to me every day in Tartarus."

She kissed his face, his lips, his ear. "I've missed your skin."

"Mmm." He returned her kisses. "So have I."

"We'll see you two lovebirds later," Cubie said.

"Why?' Clifford barked.

"They need their privacy," Galin explained. "And they're making me a little sick."

Clifford reluctantly followed the black Doberman pinscher and fluffy polecat out of the bat cave.

"We'll catch up with you in a minute," Therese called after them.

Thanatos put his hands on Therese's abdomen. "Wow. The twins have grown a lot in one week."

"They've missed your touch."

He kissed her gently on the lips and then knelt on the ground, even though it was damp and dirty, and kissed her swollen belly.

Together they walked through the winding tunnel along the Phelgethon back toward their rooms.

Than seemed distracted, so Therese asked, "Are you feeling okay?"

He squeezed her hand. "I should ask the same of you."

"Fine but…"

"What?" Than's frown made her stomach lurch.

"It's time," Therese said before they had reached their part of the palace.

Than looked down at her. His mouth dropped open. "So soon?"

She laughed and said, "Not the twins, silly. It's time to confront your father about Pete and Melinoe."

Than let out his breath. "I still don't think there's anything Hades can do without Melinoe's cooperation."

"There has to be," she insisted. "Please?"

He sighed. "Lead the way."

At the door to Hades's chamber, Therese and Than heard shouting.

"McAdams has moved on to the Elysian Fields," Tizzie snapped.

Therese shuddered. The man who had killed her parents had moved on, already?

"And your point?" Hades snapped back.

"If someone like that killer can be purged of wrong-doing and have a chance at redemption," Tizzie said, "then why can't Pete?"

"You know the rules!"

"But Pete was only using his gifts for good. He should be allowed a chance!"

"That's not what you want, and you know it!"

"I do too, Father! I want him to be happy, even at the expense of my own happiness!"

"There's nothing I can do," Hades replied. "Now leave me be!"

Tizzie rushed from the door, her snake hair hissing.

Therese swallowed hard and turned to Than. "Maybe this isn't the right time."

"For what?" Hades demanded from inside. "Enter!"

***

Jen froze on the bottom step when she heard the voice of Mr. Stern at the front door. She'd been napping after a late night of babysitting Lynn for Carol and Richard. Peering around the corner, she saw her mother leaning against the open door with a cigarette in a shaky hand. Her gray hair had recently been cut in its usual bowl shape for the funeral, but it was stringy and in need of a wash.

"I'm sorry, John," Jen's mother said. "I just can't do this right now."

"Don't shut me out."

"I need time."

"Believe me, Steph. I know how you feel," Mr. Stern said.

"Will you please stop saying that?" Jen's mom said in a raised voice. "Please quit saying you know how I feel! You *don't* know how I feel! Now please go!"

Jen jumped at the slam of the door. Then she softly crept back upstairs to her room and fell on her bed and cried.

Her poor mother! She would never be the same.

Jen wiped her eyes and reached for her dream globe. More than ever she needed Hip. Things had been strained between them lately, for reasons she didn't quite understand, but he had visited her a few nights ago and had admitted he loved her.

At first she had thought he was a figment, but when she had said the words Therese had taught her to say ("Figment, I command you to show yourself!), he hadn't turned into one of the giggling eel-like creatures that had often left her feeling disappointed. The person who had said he loved her had been the real Hypnos.

If it hadn't been for her sadness over losing Pete and her concern for her mother, Jen would be on cloud nine. Hip made her feel so happy to be alive, in spite of all the tragedy that surrounded her family recently. There was something about his playful charm and easy grace—not to mention his magnificent good looks—that lifted her up no matter how often she fell down in the dumps. Maybe he could lift her up again.

She closed her eyes and asked to see him. He appeared immediately, but he wasn't alone. Standing beside him looking smitten was his old fiancé. And they were holding hands.

"Hip?" Jen asked. "What's going on?"

Hip's eyes widened as he looked directly at her through the globe. "Jen?"

Jen stared at the globe with disbelief. Her throat tightened, her mouth went dry, and everything around her went still, as though time had stopped. Was this really happening? She tried to speak.

She opened her mouth, but nothing came out.

"Jen, I…"

"F-figment! I command you to show yourself!" she finally said through her tight throat.

"Jen…"

"Figment! Figment!"

"I'm no figment."

Jen climbed from her bed with the globe cradled like a football in one arm. Then she flung her window open and tossed the globe from her second-floor bedroom as far as she could. She watched it hit the ground and shatter into pieces, just like her heart. Iridescent light flickered from it like a dying flame and then disappeared. She closed the window and returned to her bed, trying not to cry as she hugged her pillow, but the tears came hard.

I'm such an idiot, she thought. How had she ever believed a god could love her?

"Therese!" Jen prayed. "Please come as soon as you can. If you're still my friend, I need you!"

Chapter Three: Unexpected Visits

As Than followed Therese into his father's chambers, Therese turned to him with a look of concern.

Jen is calling to me, she prayed. *It sounds like an emergency.*

Go. I'll handle my father.

Than walked across the room and explained why Therese had vanished.

"What brings you here?" Hades asked. "I doubt you've come to keep me company, knowing how miserable I am with your mother away."

"I should have come for that." A wave of guilt washed over Than. "I've only just returned from Tartarus, and I have a lot on my mind."

"Take a seat and tell me about it." Hades motioned to a chair, not far from his. "It doesn't seem that long ago when your mother and I were expecting our twins, and here you are, expecting yours."

Than sat but didn't reply. He didn't think his situation was similar to his father's in the least. Hades had always been a part of Than and Hip's lives. Thanatos wouldn't get that with his children.

"You're worried about them, of course," Hades said. "All parents worry. And you think because your children are mortal you have more to fear than those of us with godly children. But you couldn't be more wrong."

Than lifted his brows but said nothing, sensing his father had plenty to say.

"Your children are destined to live lives of greatness. They will shine like a bright flame, and then they will spend eternity in the Elysian Fields. Once they are there, your worries are over." Hades tugged at his beard. "My worries over my children haunt me for all of eternity. I can never escape them. Just before you came here, your sister Tisiphone asked me for something I had no power to grant. Do you know what that does to a father? It's maddening."

"What does she want?" Than asked.

"To free the new seer from Tartarus. I think what she really wants is to grant him the status of a god."

"Impossible?"

Hades frowned. "Not impossible. Deals can be made. But the Fates require a trade, like they did with old Admetus centuries ago. Remember? Which of us would trade places with the seer and spend eternity in Tartarus? I know none, do you?"

Than shook his head. No god in his or her right mind would choose to spend eternity in Tartarus. "What if Pete were sent to the Fields of Elysium—forgiven for his pride. He did help us, after all."

"It's against the rules," Hades said. "The ancient law forbids it."

"But…"

"And even if we could find some way around the ancient law—something I highly doubt—that would only worsen your sister's situation. At least with the boy in Tartarus, she can have a relationship with him. If he were to pass on to the fields—well, you know what happens to souls who pass on."

"They lose their memories."

"Not to mention their free will."

Than rubbed his forehead. He hadn't been back in his body long, and the transition was never without some pain. He wished he could go to sleep.

"That, of course, would be better for the seer, but not for your sister."

"What of Melinoe?" Than asked. "Couldn't she be freed from Tartarus? It seems unfair that she should be condemned when she had so much going against her."

"We are all responsible for our choices," Hades said.

"But she was used, manipulated, and…"

Suddenly they were startled by a ruckus from somewhere above them.

"Let me through!" a voice bellowed.

Hades jumped to his feet. "Poseidon?"

"Release the wards on your abominable palace and let me inside!" Poseidon's voice called.

Hades motioned his hand about the room, and Poseidon practically fell from the ceiling, landing squarely on his feet. He was breathing heavily and was drenched in sea water.

"What brings you here?" Hades asked.

Than climbed to his feet and stared dumbly at Poseidon's unexpected entry.

"My wife and my trident have been stolen from me," Poseidon said. "I've just escaped, and barely at that."

***

Therese found Jen in her upstairs bedroom, face down on her bed and sobbing into her pillow.

"Jen? What's wrong?" Therese asked.

Jen was so startled by Therese's sudden arrival that she cleared half a foot before landing on her belly again.

"Oh, thank the gods you're here!" Jen said, sitting up and slouching with a pathetic-looking frown and red, tear-stained cheeks. Do you have any idea why that Pa*SHIT*ia is holding hands with Hip?"

Therese's mouth dropped open. What in the world was Jen talking about? "Well, first of all, like I've told you before, it's Pa*sith*ea."

"Oh, that's right. Like the dark lord of the Sith. I knew there was another reason I didn't like her. She's pure evil."

Therese rolled her eyes. "They were holding hands? I'm sure there's an explanation. Hip is *not* interested in her anymore. Jen, it's been *centuries*."

"Well, *she's* still interested in *him*, I can tell you that. I saw the look on her face in the dream globe clear as day."

"So it was a dream?" Therese asked, even more confused than before.

"No. Well, they were in the dream world—that's how I could see them. But they weren't figments."

"Are you sure?"

Jen threw herself on her pillow again and screamed.

"Calm down. I'm sorry. Listen, there must be some explanation. I can't believe you called me all the way over here from a very important meeting because you're feeling insecure about Hip."

Jen leapt from the bed and gave Therese the evil eye. "Well, we can't all be goddesses!"

Therese's eyebrows lifted as Jen's angry expression crumpled into another round of tears.

"That's not the worst of it! My mom...she..." Jen threw herself on her pillow again and screamed.

Therese rolled her eyes and tried to recall if she had ever acted this way when she was mortal. She was sure she must have, but, thankfully, she couldn't remember it. "What's wrong with your mom?"

She could barely understand Jen as she said into the pillow, "She and Mr. Stern had a thing going. She was happy. Now she's breaking his heart along with her own." Jen turned her head to the side and sought Therese's face. Jen looked like she was possessed, like the character in *The Exorcist*, when she added, "You *have* to take my mom to Tartarus to see Pete. It's the only way!"

"What? That's impossible. Hades will never go for that."

Jen sat up on the edge of her bed. "Why not? What's the good of having a best friend who's a goddess if she can't do me a little favor? You're the reason we're all in this mess!"

Therese took a step back, her chin nearly hitting the floor. Did Jen really blame Therese for Pete's death?

"If you hadn't fallen for Than, you'd probably be married to Pete right now and we'd all be living happily ever after."

"You can't be serious."

"Are you saying I'm wrong?"

Tears pricked Therese's eyes. "You think Pete's dead because of me."

Jen slammed her hands on the bed. "Not exactly. Now don't you start crying, too. We'll drown. I didn't mean what I said. It's not your fault. But surely you can get me in to see Pete. Promise me you'll try."

Therese wiped her eyes and nodded. "Okay. I promise."

"And can you please see if you can find out what's going on between Hip and Pa*shit*ia? I mean the evil Sith lord?"

Therese managed a smile. "Yes. I'll look into it."

***

Hip soared through the sky with Pasithea in his arms. He'd forgotten how much he had once loved her, and he'd forgotten how good it felt to be in her arms. She was so beautiful—the most beautiful creature alive.

"Oh, Darling," Pasithea said in her sweet voice.

He'd forgotten just how sweet. He brushed her lips with his.

The light touch turned into a deeper kiss that brought chills of delight to the back of his neck. He wanted to marry her now, or as soon as possible.

"Be my wife and make me the happiest god in existence," he said to her.

"I've never stopped loving you," she said in her sweet voice. "And I would have waited centuries more to hear you say that."

"Why don't we go make some mortals as happy as we are?" he said with a wink.

"Let's do it!"

He grinned. "They'll never be as happy, though, will they?"

"Never!" Her eyes beamed back at him.

Together they entered the dream world to bring those who slept dreams of love.

In the middle of one particularly satisfying dream, Hip was interrupted by a prayer from Jen.

"I can't believe you're doing this to me. I thought you were different."

Hip was annoyed. He'd heard stories of gods who were plagued by the constant prayers of unrequited love by girls gone mad, but he himself had never personally experienced it. Now he wondered what he had ever seen in Jen Holt.

***

On her way back from Colorado, Therese spotted a group of shady people making money off of rooster fights. The poor roosters were angry, confused, and badly injured, but Therese evacuated the rotting building (by blowing smoke and fire into it), swept up the roosters, and carried them to safety. After healing them and calming them down, she took each to neighboring farmers where she knew they would be treated properly.

From there, Therese decided to go to Mount Olympus. Not only did she want to check on her mother-in-law, but she also had questions for Hera and Apollo. Unsure of what to do once the twins were born, she thought those two might give her guidance. Plus, she really missed Hecate, Hermes, and Aphrodite, and there was a good chance they'd be there, too.

As soon as she entered the court, Aphrodite called out to her, and the Graces rushed over and oohed and awed over Therese.

"You look so beautiful!" Algaea said, embracing her.

Algaea's hugs always reminded Therese of her mother. Hephaestus came up beside his wife with a big embrace that included the both of them, and that group hug filled Therese with a sense of home.

"Sweeeeet!" Cinny's high-pitch squeal made Therese jump. "May I touch your belly?"

Hands soon covered Therese's abdomen, and sighs and laughter echoed all around her.

"What a gorgeous mother you make!" Thalia said. "I can't wait to meet your beautiful babes!"

"Hermes and Hestia, isn't that right?" Algaea asked.

"That's right," Therese said beaming.

Thalia suddenly covered Therese's face with kisses, and Therese broke out in giggles.

"Where's Pashit—I mean Pasithea?" Therese asked as her cheeks grew red. Darn that Jen for planting that bad nickname into Therese's head!

"She's with Hypnos," Aphrodite replied. "By Zeus's orders."

Goose bumps popped up and down Therese's arms. "Zeus's orders?"

Aphrodite glanced around nervously and then whispered, "Zeus was worried about the quality of sleep people were getting while Hip moped around unhappily, so Zeus ordered Cupid to intervene."

Therese's jaw dropped open. "Does Hip love Pasithea now?"

Aphrodite nodded. "But it's not right. We've got to do something."

Before Therese could ask more, Hermes came up from behind and said, "I hope you plan on saying hello to the rest of us."

Therese whipped around and wrapped her arms around the messenger god's neck. She'd never forget that he was the one responsible for saving the lives of her twins. "Of course. I even brought my flute." She pulled it out of thin air, just as she had once done in a dream the first time she had met the sons of Hades.

"Wonderful!" Hermes said. "I'll grab my pipe and join you."

The Graces clapped their hands with excitement, and Aphrodite smiled with approval.

As Therese crossed the great room, she stopped in the center and politely bowed before Hera and Zeus. Then she turned and did the same to Rhea. When she saw Hecate visiting with Hestia, she went to them and hugged them both. She noticed Persephone and Demeter weren't there, so she sent a prayer to them. They entered from Demeter's rooms at once with huge smiles on their faces and open arms.

"I've come to play a concert," Therese said to them and to all the other gods in the room.

Everyone applauded, including Ares, who appeared from the back at the rainbow steps just as Therese made her announcement.

"Well, well," Ares said as he strolled across the court. "If it isn't the goddess of animal companions. And how are you doing these days with two buns in the oven, no less?"

"Fine, thank you," she lied, hiding her trembling hands. She wished the god of war didn't make her so nervous. Plus it freaked her out every time she looked at him and realized his hair color was identical to hers. His blood ran through her, but to think of it made hers boil. "And you?"

"Better than you, I'll wager."

"Why's that?" she dared to ask.

"Because I'm not being forced to choose between my children and the love of my life."

Therese turned beet red—redder than their hair.

"That is essentially what it's all coming down to for you, isn't it?" Ares said.

"There's still a lot to be worked out," Therese stammered.

Aphrodite stepped forward. "She's come to play us a concert. Let's not ruin it with complicated thoughts."

"Of course, my dear," Ares said. "No one's ever accused you of having complicated thoughts."

"Excuse me?" Aphrodite asked. "You must not hope to accompany me on my next trip to Paris."

Hephaestus took Aphrodite's arm and escorted her back to her chair near the Graces as he said, "You can't blame a god of war for introducing conflict whenever he gets the chance. Don't take it personally. Your beauty is complicated enough."

"A concert, eh?" Ares asked Therese when the flames of his fire had been quelled by the god of the forge.

Therese realized at that moment that Hephaestus knew exactly how to play Ares. "I was hoping Hermes and Apollo would join me," Therese added, no longer confident of performing on her own. "Is Apollo at home?"

Artemis stepped forward. "He'll be here shortly. Why don't you start without him?"

So Therese took a seat beside Hermes and the two of them played her favorite Handel Sonata, which always made her think of her parents. She sent a prayer to them where they sat in the elm watching over Carol, Richard, and Lynn.

Before she and Hermes had gotten to the end of the song, Apollo did indeed arrive, and he took out his lyre and joined them.

Chapter Four: Breaking News

Than was grateful his father hadn't asked him to leave as Poseidon explained in further detail what had happened.

"Ever since Zeus and the Alliance declared Amphitrite my equal ruler of the sea, she has wanted to use my trident to pay back Scylla for all her abuses against her."

"They've never been very fond of one another," Hades agreed.

"My wife can't swim through the Messina Straight without getting attacked by that monstrous crab," Poseidon added.

Than had had plenty of encounters with Scylla. With her six long necks and grisly heads and her twelve tentacle legs, she lurched from her cave and snapped her crab pincers at him every chance she got.

"So Scylla has Amphitrite and your trident?" Than asked.

"Of course not," Poseidon said. "I agreed with the Alliance to grant my wife equal authority over the sea, but I never said I would share the trident."

"Then what happened?" Hades asked.

"I must have a spy among my court," Poseidon said. "Because when I accompanied my wife to have her revenge on Scylla, we were ambushed."

A spy? In Poseidon's castle? Than recalled the many merfolk who dwelled there and mentally checked for motives, but he came up empty.

"By whom?" Hades asked.

"I don't know."

"Couldn't you see your attackers?" Than asked.

Poseidon raised his hands in the air. "All of the monsters of the sea were there—Scylla, Charybdis, and Echidna—plus the Chimera and Ladon."

"From Hera's garden?" Than asked. He shuddered at the memory of what he had done to that one-hundred-headed serpent.

"That's the one," Poseidon replied. "Which is why I came here instead of Mount Olympus. Ladon is like a puppy to Hera, and he takes his post very seriously."

"So you think Hera, and by extension Zeus, is behind the abduction?" Hades asked.

"I don't know what to think," Poseidon admitted. "But Phorcys has always favored Zeus over me, and those were his children in the attack."

"Couldn't the Old Man of the Sea be operating without Zeus and Hera?" Than asked. "Maybe he wants to regain control of the waters."

Poseidon shook his head. "Phorcys and Keto and all of their children don't have enough power combined to overtake me, or they would have done so already. As it was, Amphitrite and I defeated every one of the monsters in the ambush before a paralyzing wave temporarily stunned us. That's when my trident was taken. I couldn't move. Somebody more powerful than Phorcys and Keto is working with them. I'm telling you, it felt like I'd been struck by a lightning bolt. If not Zeus, then who?"

"But what would motivate our brother to betray you?" Hades asked.

"Perhaps he's bitter about our allegiance to the Athena Alliance, and this is his way of paying us back," Poseidon said.

"Us?" Hades picked at his beard.

"You may be next."

Than's mind raced to Therese and their babies. *Where are you?* He prayed to her.

***

The Muses sang along and the Graces danced to the beautiful music created by Apollo, Hermes, and Therese. It was clear no one—not even Zeus—wanted the fun to end; but, when they finished the fifth song, Therese put away her flute and said she had to get back to work. Than had been praying for her return. Something was up in the Underworld. Between Than's prayers and Jen's, Therese could barely concentrate. She let Than know she would soon be leaving Mount Olympus.

After the objections and then the resigned applause had died down and everyone had gone back to their business, Therese crossed the room to Hera.

"May I speak privately with you for a moment, Lady Hera?" Therese asked.

The co-ruler of the sky stepped from her throne, clearly happy to have been singled out, and walked with Therese to the dining hall where Hestia was busy laying out a beautiful table spread.

"Your music was lovely," the goddess of the hearth said to Therese, before returning to the kitchen.

"Thank you." Therese blushed. She hadn't spoken much with Hestia since their stand against Zeus, but an opportunity never seemed to present itself.

"What's on your mind?" Hera asked Therese when they were alone again.

They sat at the end of the long table as Therese told Hera what Pete had said about the twins. "What should I do?" Therese asked when she had finished. "Should I renounce my duties and return to the Upperworld to raise our children? I don't see any other way."

"You can't renounce your duties without going half-mad," Hera said. "You've seen what happens to Demeter each fall and winter, and what has happened to Dionysus."

Therese wondered if Hera realized her role in Dionysus's choice to stay away from the other gods. "I guess I could perform my duties at night, while the children sleep."

Hera frowned. "I know this would be hard for a mother to do, but the best thing for the twins would be to give them up to be raised by mortals."

The room spun. Therese gripped the edge of the table and broke out in a sweat. "You can't be serious."

"But I am."

"You want me to give up my babies?" She thought she might be sick as she hugged her belly.

"I don't *want* you to do anything. I'm merely telling you what would be best for the children."

"Why wouldn't being with their mother be best for them?" As Therese stood, she clutched the back of the chair for balance. Maybe she shouldn't listen to this goddess. What was she thinking in coming to Hera for help?

"Mortals need to live with other mortals. Imagine how confusing it would be for your son and daughter to know they were children of gods—to know that you will live forever and they won't. As they grow old, you and Thantatos will continue to look young. They would be better off not knowing you. It's your choice, of course." Hera also stood. "I'm sorry. I truly am."

"How long before they're born?' Therese asked. "Nine months?"

"No one knows," Hera said. "Every goddess is different. Some have carried babies for many months. For others, it's been weeks, sometimes days."

Therese's eyes widened. "What? But it won't be anytime soon will it?"

Hera shrugged. "I wish I knew."

Hera left Therese alone in the dining room.

As Therese stood clutching the chair and holding back tears, Hestia entered and said, "I didn't mean to eavesdrop, but I couldn't help overhearing. I'm so sorry, Therese."

"Do you agree with Hera?" Therese asked. "Do you think she's right about me giving up the babies?"

Hestia took a deep breath and nodded.

Therese stumbled from the room. She needed to rein in her tears so she could visit her mother-in-law. Not to do so would appear rude. She had just entered Demeter's rooms when Than's prayer came to her suddenly: *Get out of there now.*

Therese god travelled from Demeter's arms to Than's side in his father's chambers.

Persephone and Demeter's prayers of concern assailed Therese as she travelled. She would tell them what was going on, as soon as she knew herself.

"What's wrong?" she asked Than, surprised to see Poseidon with him and Hades. "Why did you call me from Mount Olympus?"

They filled her in on what had happened to Poseidon, Amphitrite, and the trident.

Poseidon said, "Therese needs to return immediately. Don't you see? Maybe she could learn something."

Therese covered her belly in an automatic, protective gesture. When it was only her own well-being, she never hesitated to risk it; but things were different now.

"With all due respect," Than said, "I'd rather not put my wife and children in danger. We can send someone else to spy on Mount Olympus."

"But they trust her," Poseidon said.

"What were you doing there?" Hades asked.

Therese glanced nervously at Than. She hadn't wanted him to know how badly she struggled with what to do about their twins, but she couldn't lie to Hades. "I went to ask Hera and Apollo for their advice."

Hades frowned. "Concerning?"

Therese stared at the floor. "What to do about the babies, with them being mortal and all."

"And did you ask them?" Hades prompted.

"I asked Hera."

"And what did she say?" Hades picked at his beard and waited for her reply.

Tears welled in her eyes as she looked at Than and said, "She thinks we should give them up."

"What?" Than's mouth fell open. "No. Never!"

"Hestia agrees," Therese said as the floodgates opened and tears rushed down her cheeks. She sucked in her lips, trying to hold back the sobs, but they broke through and shook her violently. "They both think it's best for mortals to be raised by mortals."

Than put his arms around her.

She completely lost control of herself in his arms as the words tumbled from her lips. "And Hera says that if I renounce my duties as a god to live in the Upperworld, I'll go half-mad, like Demeter and Dionysus." She bit her lips, fighting to regain control. "What are we going to do?"

"Clearly she's in no shape to spy on Mount Olympus," Than said, without letting go of her. "Think of another plan."

"Zeus would never harm the babies," Hades said.

"He tried to swallow her just a few weeks ago," Than argued.

"He didn't know about the twins—or the prophecy." Hades crossed his arms. "None of us knew."

"You knew," Therese said.

"I knew there would be a set of twins, but I never imagined they'd be yours," Hades said.

That stung, but Therese fought to hide her hurt.

Hades continued, "Now that he knows *your twins* will restore faith in Mount Olympus, why would Zeus want to interfere with that?"

"He's right," Poseidon said. "Therese is the best person for this mission. They trust her, and they won't want to harm the babes. Plus, she was just there. Send her back to ask around.

Wanting to spend time with her mother-in-law is a sound motive, too."

"I did hope to speak with Zeus about Melinoe," Therese admitted.

"Zeus has no say about my realm!" Hades objected. "Now off with you!"

Than shook his head. "For all we know, Zeus could imprison her and take our babies away from us. He might have plans for them. We don't know!"

"Do you have any better ideas?" Poseidon shouted.

"Yes," Than said calmly. "Send me."

***

As the sun set behind the mountains in Colorado, Jen turned the last of the horses out to pasture and headed indoors to wash up. Her mother had already gone ahead of her to the kitchen to reheat the leftovers for dinner. Bobby was finishing up in the barn. Jen couldn't wait to get out of her clothes, into a hot shower, and then go straight to bed. She didn't even want to eat. She wanted to go to sleep, where she didn't have to think and feel.

She was aware of how ironic it was that she had once been eager to sleep for the opposite reasons, but she refused to think about Hip. *Stop!* she commanded herself. *He's moved on. You have to do the same.*

When she opened her bedroom door, Jen found Hip's sister Tizzie sitting on her bed. She was wearing black silk pants and a silver halter top. Emeralds hung around her neck and dangled from her earlobes. Her long, curly black hair fell across her bare shoulders. Jen had forgotten how beautiful she was.

"Therese sent me," the Fury said. "I'm to take you and your mother to Tartarus for a visit."

Jen covered her mouth with both hands. This was exactly what she had wanted, but now that it was about to happen, she was scared to death.

She and Tizzie walked downstairs to the kitchen.

"Mom?" Jen called. "You remember Than's sister, Tizzie, don't you?"

"My goodness!" Mrs. Holt cried. "When did you arrive, dear?"

"Just a few moments ago," Tizzie said.

"You look so lovely. I'm sorry we're not fancier around here. Would you like to have dinner with us? It's nothing special. Left over steak and potatoes and steamed brussel sprouts."

Jen glanced at the Fury and doubted she was interested in eating leftovers. "Mom, there's um, something I need to tell you."

"It can wait until after dinner," Tizzie said with a hint of red in her eyes. "I would love to dine with you. Thank you for the invitation."

Bobby walked in at that moment but stopped dead in his tracks when he saw their visitor.

"Hey, Tizzie," he said once the shock had worn off. "How's Therese and the rest of your family?"

"Oh, things are a bit hectic right now, especially with Therese and Than's twins on the way."

Bobby's chin nearly hit the floor.

"Therese is pregnant with twins?" Mrs. Holt asked. "When is she due?"

"I don't know," Tizzie's face turned a shade of red, and Jen could have sworn a snake appeared in her hair. "You didn't know she was expecting?"

"No," Mrs. Holt said, frowning at Jen. "But that's wonderful news. Carol and Richard must be thrilled."

"I think it's a secret," Jen explained.

Bobby and Jen washed their hands and face at the kitchen sink while their mother laid the food out on the table. Jen put out plates, napkins, and silverware, and Bobby made a pitcher of iced tea. Then they all sat down and ate.

Uncomfortable with the silence, Jen said to Bobby, "Mom and I are going to take a walk with Tizzie after dinner, but we'll be right back."

"Bobby can come, too, if he'd like," Tizzie said.

"What?" Jen couldn't believe it. "Are you sure?"

"Of course," the Fury said. "As long as he knows how to keep a secret."

"No one would believe him anyway," Jen said, chuckling. Surreal was the only word she could think of to describe this whole evening.

"What are you talking about?" Bobby asked. "A walk where?"

Jen glanced at Tizzie, not sure how to break the news. "Mom, remember what I told you the other day, about going to see Pete?"

Bobby dropped his fork, and it clattered against his plate.

"Not now," Mrs. Holt said. "Let's not talk that way in front of our guest."

"It's okay to talk about Pete in front of me, Mrs. Holt," Tizzie said kindly. "I'm in love with him, and I've come to tell you he and I plan to be married."

Jen was so shocked that she almost didn't catch her mother when Mrs. Holt fainted. Bobby turned white.

Jen said, "Don't you faint, too."

"Do you think your mother doesn't like me?" Tizzie asked as snakes rose from her head. "I really want her to like me."

Jen could think of nothing to say as she stared dumbly back at Tizzie and her wild, snaky hair. Jen fanned her mother, trying to bring her back to consciousness.

***

Hip and Pasithea flew above the clouds and back to the gates of Mount Olympus, where they ran into Thanatos.

"What brings you here, bro'?" Hip asked, as he slid an arm around his beautiful companion.

Hip could tell Than was surprised to see him with his old fiancé after so many centuries had passed since he had last held her in his arms.

"Hip?" he asked. "What's going on?"

"Pasithea and I are a couple again," Hip said.

"We're going to be married," Pasithia added.

What about Jen, Than prayed.

Hip shrugged and said out loud, "What about her? Things change." Hip couldn't be blamed if his amazing good looks made women fall in love with him.

I don't know what you're up to, but we'll talk more about that later, Than prayed. *For now you should know that I'm here to spy on Zeus and Hera. Poseidon's wife and trident have been stolen, and Poseidon suspects they're behind it.*

Hip frowned. "But why?"

Let's not discuss it in front of others.

"You can trust Pasithea," Hip said. "Before you go inside to spy on Zeus and Hera, tell me everything you know."

"That *is* everything I know," Than said before turning to the gates with a frown. "Winter, Summer, Spring, and Fall, open the gates so that I…"

Before Than finished the request, Hip felt a crushing blow to his back. He fell to his knees as Pasithea's scream rose sharply above him. His skin felt tight, his muscles stiff, and his heart heavy.

When he could finally speak, he turned to Pasithea and asked, "What's happening?" His voice sounded funny—more like a bray.

Pasithea shed tears as she gazed down at him. "You're an ass!"

Hip blinked. Why would she say such a thing after their glorious afternoon together? He looked down at his hands and nearly fell over. His hands and feet had become hooves. Gray fur covered his body. He was, indeed, quite literally, an ass!

"Thanatos," Hip said, though it came out like a bray. "Help me!"

Than's eyes were fixed on the clouds. "Therese?"

Hip followed his brother's gaze in time to see an arrow heading straight for him. In his donkey body, he lacked the grace to dodge the blow, and the arrow struck him, full in the heart. As soon as it did, the gravity of his situation also struck him. He looked at Pasithea in horror. He had just spent the past few days loving her with all his heart, but it hadn't been real. Sure, he had old feelings for her and had always loved her to some extent, but his heart really and truly belonged to Jen Holt. His throat tightened as he recalled how Jen had looked at him and Pasithea through the dream globe. He now tried to reach out to Jen through the globe, but found only emptiness.

"Where's Jen?" he brayed, feeling panic coming on.

"She's with Tizzie in Tartarus," Therese replied.

"What?" Hip bucked his back legs in the air instinctively. He hadn't meant to do it. This donkey body seemed to have a mind of its own. "Why? What happened?"

"She and Bobby and her mother are visiting Pete," Therese explained.

Relief swept over Hip like a warm wave of sunshine. For a moment, he had thought she was dead and he was too late. He *hee-hawed* his relief, though a visit by mortals was still pretty weird.

Therese struck him with another arrow, and pressure gripped him all over as he transformed back into his natural form. Thank goodness Therese had the ability to transform a god. She hadn't been able to change Pete back from a golden retriever, but she'd saved Hip from being an everlasting ass.

Than clapped a hand on Hip's shoulder. "So you were pierced by Cupid. That explains a lot."

"Oh, hell," Hip said, combing his fingers through his dark blonde hair. It was a relief to have it back again.

Therese flew closer to him and said, "I'm sorry. I didn't mean to hurt you."

"Hypnos?" Pasithea squeaked. "Are you alright?"

"Oh, boy," he muttered. Was he in a real mess now, or what?

Chapter Five: Over and Under

As soon as Than entered the court on Mount Olympus, his mother flew at him, demanding to know what had happened to Therese.

"She never explained," Persephone said. "I've been worried sick."

Than told his mother through prayer what had happened, so others wouldn't overhear. This did him no good, however, because not long after he and his mother joined Demeter and Hecate, Pasithea rushed through the room, pointing her finger at him, squealing, "Spy! Spy!"

All eyes turned on Thanatos.

Zeus stood up from his throne. "Now, Pasithea. Be careful of false accusations."

Pasithia stopped in the center of the room, tears flowing down her face like a fountain. She trembled and sought out Aphrodite, who returned her gaze with a frown.

"What is the meaning of this?" Aphrodite asked her.

"I heard Thanatos and Hypnos talking outside the gates," the Grace began. "Hypnos asked Thanatos why he had come to spy on Zeus and Hera."

"Apollo?" Zeus turned to the god of light. "Does this Grace speak the truth?"

"I'm afraid so," Apollo said, before asking Than through prayer what was going on.

Than knew he couldn't lie to Apollo, so he prayed back with what had transpired between the monsters of the sea and Poseidon and his wife. He also explained why he had come to Mount Olympus. *Poseidon said it felt like a lightning bolt.*

"Where is Hypnos now?" Zeus asked, unaware of the conversation between Than and Apollo.

Pasithea covered her face and was wracked with sobs, barely managing to utter, "He flew off to find Jen Holt!"

"But he was struck with the arrow of Eros!" Zeus bellowed. "How is this possible? He should never wish to leave your side! Did you do something to offend him?"

Pasithea fell on her knees, shaking her head, completely at a loss. Aphrodite went to her and helped her back to her feet and comforted her by stroking her hair.

"Hermes! Bring me Cupid!" Zeus commanded.

Ares strolled to the center of the court near Pasithea and Aphrodite. "I've seen an arrow of Eros neutralized one other time," Ares said haughtily. "And it was done by the goddess of animal companions when she transformed Pete Holt into a dog."

Hermes and Cupid appeared, but Zeus had turned his attention to Than. "Where's your wife?"

"The Underworld," Than replied.

"Did she do this?" the lord of the sky asked.

"Yes," Than replied, his throat suddenly tight. He sent a prayer to Therese to go to Hades for protection immediately.

"How dare she undermine my authority!" Zeus declared. "I am still the lord of the gods! Am I not?"

At that moment Rhea stepped forward, spreading her manly hands wide. "This was to be a more democratic court, remember?" She dropped her arms to her side. "Yet you sought no one's counsel when you had Cupid pierce Hypnos's heart."

"Are you defending Therese's treason against me?" Zeus, who might explode any minute from anger, asked his mother.

"You are not a sovereign king," Rhea said boldly. "You are our leader. There's a difference."

Zeus shook his fists and shouted, "A leader who can't trust his people!"

"Has there ever been trust among us?" Demeter asked. "We all have our own agendas and operate accordingly, do we not?"

"We don't have the right to undermine Zeus," Ares insisted. "She should be punished for what she has done."

"Zeus did have his reasons," Hera added.

Than prayed to Athena to return as soon as possible. Maybe she could bring order to the chaos breaking up around them.

"Every new system has its growing pains," Hephaestus offered amiably. "We just need to work out the kinks and weld together a few cracks."

"I don't want a new system," Zeus said. "I prefer the old."

"Of course you do," Hera said.

Poseidon entered the court with a raised fist. "Is that why you stole my trident?"

***

Jen and Bobby followed their mother, Tizzie, and a white wolf down the freezing cold path to Tartarus. A river of fire illuminated the cavern, but it gave off no heat. Jen's teeth chattered, and her knees felt weak. She reached her hand out for Bobby's, and for once, he didn't bat it away, but clung to it.

They reached a huge, heavy, iron gate. It screeched against the cavern floor and ceiling as Tizzie pulled it ajar. A current of even colder air lifted up from the dark pit below.

As they broached the gate, Jen and Bobby exchanged looks of fear.

"You okay?" Jen asked Bobby.

Her mother turned a white face back to Jen, lifted her brows, but said nothing.

"Pinch me," Bobby said. "Tell me this isn't a dream."

Jen never turned down an opportunity to pinch her little brother.

"Ow!" he said, slapping her arm. "That was a figure of speech."

They turned a corner where the river of fire ended, and all below was in utter darkness.

"What in the world?" Mrs. Holt exclaimed when Tizzie started glowing.

"So you can see," Tizzie explained. "I'm trying to help you, Mrs. Holt. Now follow me, please."

They came to a large opening lined with boulders. Draping over the boulders were white, iridescent flowers Jen had only ever seen here in the Underworld. She'd forgotten what Hip had called them.

"Asphodel," Tizzie said, patting her wolf on the head.

"What?" Jen stopped short. "Can you read my mind?"

"No, of course not," Tizzie said, her snaky hair rising and falling with a huff. "You asked me, and I answered."

They continued around the corner, Jen shaking her head in disbelief. Had she asked Tizzie? She guessed she had without realizing it.

"Mom?" Pete appeared from around a corner.

His face had no eyeballs in it, and his whole body was see-through. Jen ran up to him and threw her arms around his neck, but she fell through him. He was nothing but colored air.

"Pete?" Mrs. Holt burst into tears. "Son, is that really you?"

"It's really me."

Mrs. Holt stumbled. Tizzie caught her and helped her to sit on a nearby rock.

"I need a cigarette," Mrs. Holt muttered.

Jen went to her mother's side. "You alright?"

"What happened to your eyes?" Mrs. Holt frowned at Pete.

"It's a long story," Pete said.

"I miss your beautiful face." Jen's mother batted tears from her face.

"Hi, Bobby," Pete said.

Bobby took a step back.

"Don't be scared," Pete added.

"I'm not scared," Bobby insisted. "It's just hard to look at you."

Tizzie brought a pair of sunglasses out of thin air and put them on Pete's face. "Is that better?" she asked.

"Much," Jen said.

"My poor son," Mrs. Holt said. "I've missed you so much. God, I've missed you!"

Bobby moved closer to Pete. "Are you for real?"

"Yes," Pete said. "It's really me."

Bobby's eyes widened. "This isn't a dream?"

"No." Pete took another step toward his little brother.

"And you're okay?" Bobby asked.

"I am now that I'm with Tizzie." Pete smiled at the Fury.

"Is Daddy down here, too?" Bobby asked.

"No," Tizzie answered. "His soul is still lost."

"What does that mean?" Jen asked.

"It's a long story," Pete said.

"Well, we have time, baby boy," Mrs. Holt said. "Let's hear it."

"Not all souls make it here," Pete said. "Am I right, Tizzie?"

"Yes." The Fury stood beside Pete. "Melinoe and other malevolent entities will entice some spirits with lies. If they aren't judged and sentenced, they aren't bound here."

"What happens to them?" Mrs. Holt asked.

"They usually haunt the places where they last lived. Once they're lost, they can never be brought back here. They wander the earth forever."

"That's so sad," Bobby said. "Daddy will never have peace."

Jen didn't say what she was thinking, but a part of her was glad he would have to suffer—for a while, at least.

"Can't we pray for him or something?" Mrs. Holt asked.

Tizzie shrugged. "I suppose you could pray to Hades, but I'm not sure what he could do."

"Tell me what happened to your eyes," Mrs. Holt said to Pete.

"It's easier for me to see without them," Pete explained.

"That doesn't make a lick of sense. I don't understand." Mrs. Holt stood up and moved closer to her son. "You can see me, then?"

"No, I can't," Pete said. "But I can sense you. I don't know how to explain it. I got rid of my eyes because they were getting in the way of my ability to see the future."

"You can see the future?" Jen asked.

"Not all of it," Pete replied. "Just bits and pieces."

"Can you see my future?" Jen asked.

"I might if you gave me some of your blood to drink," Pete said.

"That's disgusting." Their mother shook her head. "No blood-drinking, alright?"

But Jen didn't listen. She was so anxious to know something about her future, especially with all that had happened between her and Hip, that she slid her finger across a sharp rock and drew blood.

Pete sniffed in her direction. "Mmm."

"This is too weird," Bobby said.

"I agree," Mrs. Holt added.

Tizzie's snake hair raised in a great hiss. "Don't be rude."

Mrs. Holt and Bobby huddled together in one corner and watched in horror as Jen held up her bloody finger to Pete. Pete drank the blood with relish.

"So?" Jen asked.

Pete's head started bobbing up and down. "This makes no sense. No sense at all. No sense. No sense. No sense."

***

Therese flew on Stormy's back to the gates of Mount Olympus and asked to be let in. She took Stormy to the stables, said hello to Pegasus and the other horses there, but noticed Cupid wasn't at home. When she entered the court, she saw why. He and Hades and everyone who lived on Mount Olympus, including Athena and Metis—and even Poseidon—had assembled there. In the middle of all their shouting was her husband!

She broke through the crowd and rushed to his side where he wrapped his protective arms around her.

Zeus has accused you of committing treason against him, Than warned her through prayer.

Hades moved closer to Therese and Than, ready to defend them. Poseidon followed suit.

"It was your lightning bolt!" Poseidon said. "It wasn't the first time I have been struck!"

"How dare you accuse me!" Zeus roared.

What's going on? Therese prayed to Than, and he filled her in.

A lightning bolt? she repeated.

"I swear I had nothing to do with that attack!" Zeus continued.

"Swear on the River Styx!" Poseidon insisted.

"I swear on the River Styx!" Zeus repeated.

A lightning bolt? Therese prayed to Thanatos again. Then, out loud, she shouted, "Wait! I have an idea!"

64

Than lifted his eyebrows and asked, "What are you doing?"

Everyone's eyes were on the two of them.

Therese stepped past Poseidon and faced Zeus.

Zeus pointed a finger at her and said, "You have some nerve coming before me after going behind my back and undoing my work."

"Some of Polyphemus's sheep still have your lightning bolts sewn inside their bellies. They weren't all killed on my wedding day."

Zeus's eyes looked about to bulge from their sockets as his face took on a pale red and his brows lifted into his hair line. "What? How is that possible?"

Therese's knees felt weak, but she stood tall and narrowed her eyes. "As the goddess of animal companions, it was my duty to save them."

Zeus held her in a stare-down for many seconds, while the room remained deadly quiet. Once his rage had subsided, he said, "That was very irresponsible."

He didn't clarify which of their actions he was referring to: her act of saving the sheep or his of planting the lightning bolts inside of them. In her opinion, it was definitely the latter, but she knew better than to express it now.

"This means anyone could have been behind the attack on Poseidon," Hades said.

"But who else would have motive?" Poseidon pointed out.

Persephone rushed to her husband's side. "Aside from the lightning bolt, what made you suspect Zeus?"

"Poseidon should tell the story," Hades said.

Poseidon told them all about Ladon's part, and Hera winced.

"My poor Ladon!" she cried. "Who would put him up to this?"

Ever since Than had slaughtered Ladon, Therese had felt sorry for the one-hundred-headed serpent. He'd only been doing his job, and he was loyal to Hera. What would provoke him to leave the garden?

"You thought I wanted to punish you!" Zeus accused Poseidon.

"What would you have thought in my place?" Poseidon said without apology. "Lightning bolt, Ladon, your history of exacting punishment."

"Now wait one minute!" The pale red of rage returned to Zeus's complexion.

"Enough!" Hades said. "Let's focus on the problem at hand. Who would benefit from the trident?"

"The Old Man of the Sea," Apollo declared.

"Is that a vision?" Zeus asked, turning to the god of light.

"No," Apollo admitted. "Only speculation."

"It would be wise to bring him in for questioning," Athena said.

"Or send someone to interrogate him," Ares said. "I volunteer."

"I think we should question Polyphemus," Therese suggested.

"He would never turn against me!" Poseidon shouted.

Therese clutched her abdomen where the twins were turning somersaults. "I only meant he might know who stole his sheep."

Poseidon calmed down and shook his head. "He's not very bright. I doubt he'll know anything."

"I have little faith in the Cyclopes," Zeus agreed. "They work and follow orders, but might not be of use to us otherwise."

But Polyphemus loves his sheep, Therese prayed rather than stated.

No one acknowledged her point.

"Everyone swear before Apollo and on the River Styx that you had nothing to do with the attack and have no knowledge of the whereabouts of Amphitrite and the trident," Zeus commanded.

Every god and goddess in the room swore.

"Process of elimination," Zeus said. "Now we confront those not in our presence until we've questioned everyone, including Phorcys and Keto. Ares?"

But what if it wasn't a god? Therese prayed to Than.

He gave her a reassuring smile. *Let's let them handle this one.*

Therese was not reassured. Everyone was wrong to discount Polyphemus as a possible witness, and as soon as she could, she was going to Cyclopes Island to pay him a visit.

Ares stepped forward. "Ready to serve."

"It would be unwise to send him alone," Metis said.

Hermes raised a hand. "I'll go."

"No," Zeus commanded. "I want you to question Dionysus. Apollo should see the Muses and the Centaurs. Artemis should call on all forest nymphs. Athena…"

"Send Thanatos with Ares," Poseidon said. "The creatures of the sea are used to his presence and ignore him."

Therese's heart skipped a beat.

Than gave her a nervous glance but said to Zeus, "Ready to serve."

***

Hypnos searched all over the Underworld and could not find his father. He went to Tartarus and found Tizzie comforting Pete, who sat slumped on a rock as though he had just ran a foot race and couldn't breathe.

"Hey," Hip said. "What's wrong with the seer?"

Tizzie's snake hair flared up and down. "He saw something that was too much for him."

"What?" Hip asked.

68

"No sense," Pete muttered with his head bowed.

"I brought Jen and her family down to see him," Tizzie explained. "Therese asked me to do it. And I wanted to do it, so don't get all in my face."

Hip took a deep breath. "How did it go?"

"Fine, until Pete drank Jen's blood right in front of the others," Tizzie explained. "They turned pale as ghosts."

"And Jen?"

"She was okay with it, actually," Tizzie said, "Until Pete started seizing."

"No sense," Pete muttered again.

"Then Melinoe came to ask me a question, and Jen and her family freaked out."

"Oh, no." Hip shook his head.

"Melinoe seemed to enjoy it," Tizzie added. "I just don't think Therese has a good case for Melinoe's redemption."

"Therese swore an oath…" Hip said.

"I was there. I know it. But the Malevolent needs a lot of work. Meg is with her now."

"Where are the Holts?"

"Alecto took them home for me a few minutes ago," Tizzie added. "I'm afraid to leave Pete alone."

Meg appeared. "Where's Father?"

Hip shrugged. "I came down to ask the same thing."

"Well, don't look at *me*," Tizzie said.

"Something weird is going on," Meg insisted as her falcon squawked. "Something's not right. Hecate and I were in the middle of a conversation about Melinoe when she cut me off and said she had to go."

"Have you tried contacting her since?" Tizzie asked.

"Of course," Meg said. "She doesn't answer me."

"Have you tried talking to Hades?" Hip asked.

"No way," Meg said. "He's obviously pretty busy if he's not at home."

Father?

Not now. In fact, come to Mount Olympus immediately.

"I've got to go," he said to his sisters and then disappeared before they objected.

As soon as Hip arrived, he was questioned by Zeus. He couldn't believe someone had the gall to capture Amphitrite and the trident. Hip swore an oath that he was not involved, but as sorry as he felt for Amphitrite, he was more concerned about finding a way to communicate in person with Jen. He'd hoped to get his father's permission to hand off his duties temporarily to someone else, like Hecate, but Hades was clearly in no mood for making deals unrelated to this most recent threat to the Olympians. Hip didn't blame him, but maybe Hip would find a way around asking his father's permission.

Therese? he prayed. *Where are you?*

Chapter Six: Scylla's Revenge

Therese returned Stormy to the Underworld stables because she worried he might be too tempting a delicacy for Polyphemus. She gave all the horses there a quick brushing and a handful of oats before flying west of Greece to the Ionian Sea.

As she neared Cyclopes Island, she saw the bright flash of Zeus's chariot descending into the ocean toward the ancient castle belonging to Phorcys and Keto. Ares and Than were on their way to question the parents of the monsters of the sea about the abduction of Amphitrite. Therese wished she had been asked to go, too, because she wanted to know what the Old Man of the Sea and his wife had to say, and because she feared for Than's safety. She hovered above the water for a moment, trying to sense Than without giving away her position. She didn't want him to know what she was up to; he would only try to stop her. And she wouldn't blame him. Going to see Polyphemus was risky. Yet she truly believed she could use the Cyclops's love for his sheep to get him to cooperate, and she wouldn't take such a risk now that she was pregnant if she didn't like her odds.

Plus, the Fates had said her twins would restore faith to humanity, so nothing bad could happen to them, right?

Just as she reached out to sense Than, he appeared before her.

"What are you doing?" he asked with a look of dread on his face.

"I'm making sure you're okay." This wasn't exactly a lie.

He smiled and kissed her. "I'm fine, but if you keep hanging around here, I'll just worry about you. Let's go home together. I'll give you a play by play of what's happening with Phorcys and Keto."

She was about to tell him her plan to visit Cyclopes Island when she noticed two boys kicking a dog on the southern coast of Italy. She sent arrows into all three beings and watched with satisfaction as they embraced, but then something strange happened: the dog turned into a third boy.

"That's odd," she said to Than. "Hold on." Shielding herself from the sight of the three using her invisibility mode, she flew down to take a closer look. She had barely landed on the beach when a fierce wind slammed against her and hurled her into the sea.

Something sharp reached up and grasped her in its clutches. As she struggled against the immovable claws, she realized she had fallen into the pincers of Scylla.

The monster dragged Therese through the water and then up from the sea into a cave along the coast. Scylla's six necks were twice as long as the Hydra's one, and her six serpent-like heads each had three rows of teeth. She also had twelve long dangling legs, like tentacles, and the heads of six yelping dogs at her waist. Two long arms with pincers shot up from the monster's sides and clamped Therese in a death hold. She tried to god travel out, but something was blocking her efforts.

The monster came to a halt and stared at her with the four center heads. Each had a single eye.

"What do you want from me?" Therese shouted, but the monster said nothing.

The cave was bright, the inner walls covered in iridescent crystals. The source of light glowed somewhere in the back of the cave. Therese strained her neck to look all around, hoping for a means of escape, when her eyes fell on a beautiful bright goddess, with bright hair and eyes beaming like the sun. She was the source of light in the cave.

"Who are you?" Therese asked as the goddess moved toward her.

"Circe," the goddess said politely. "Daughter to Helios. It's a pleasure to meet you, Therese."

"Can you help me?" Therese struggled against the claws.

All six of Scylla's heads scoffed.

"I'm afraid it is you who will help me," the goddess said.

"What can *I* do? I'm a bit stuck at the moment." Obviously Scylla and Circe were working together, but why?

Unexpectedly, Scylla said, from all six of her heads, "I used to be beautiful, like you." Her voice echoed throughout the chamber.

"Tell the truth, Scylla," Circe said in the voice of a kindergarten teacher correcting a child. "You were born that way, were you not?"

"I was," the monster said. "But Circe transformed me into a beautiful goddess, and for years I was happy!"

"Until she stole my love from me," Circe said in a voice less kind.

Scylla screeched, "I never asked for his love! It wasn't my fault! It was never my fault! Now change me! You swore an oath!"

Therese's head was spinning from the monster's fierce shrieks.

Circe moved closer to Therese and sprinkled her with a white, bitter-smelling powder. The substance landed in her hair and on her face and arms. She breathed it in by accident, causing her to sneeze.

When she had finished spreading the powder over Therese, Circe said to Scylla, "We have to wait until she's changed. Then, I shall change you."

Circe disappeared, and the cave became dark.

Therese's mouth fell open and she met one of Scylla's four eyes. "What's happening?"

"It was the only way she would change me back," Scylla said. "She set you up with the boys on the beach. She used her black magic to change one of them into a dog."

"What is this stuff? What's it going to do to me?"

"The bones of a slaughtered animal ground into a fine powder and mixed with her terrible herbs and potions."

Therese felt a panic coming on. "What's it going to do to me?" she repeated.

"It's going to turn you into this." Scylla lifted one of her pincers and motioned to herself. "So you can take my place."

"I don't believe you!" Therese shouted. "You've been deceived. How could a daughter of Helios have that kind of power?"

"Black magic," Scylla said. "It comes with a price. Circe rarely sleeps because the black magic haunts her. The ghosts of her sacrifices torment her. Her power is not a natural gift. Nevertheless, she wields it."

"This can't be happening," Therese insisted as a pressure gripped her chest.

Scylla laid her down on the floor of the cave. "Oh, but it is."

***

Thanatos dove into the sea after Therese, but Charbydis pulled him under with her powerful whirlpool. He multiplied into fifty, then a hundred, and swam against the monster's current, slowing it enough for him to escape. Once he was free, integrated, and out of the water, he could no longer sense Therese.

Where are you? He prayed. When she didn't answer, he shouted her name, again and again, causing the skies to crack with thunder.

Back in the house of Phorcys and Keto, where he sat across from his hosts, he turned to Ares, panting with panic and tears in his eyes.

Something's happened to Therese, he prayed.

Disintegrate and dispatch to Poseidon, Ares replied. *We must complete our interrogation here.*

Thanatos did as Ares said. He god travelled directly to Poseidon's palace and pounded on the door.

"So we need to know if you have any knowledge about the attack on Amphitrite and Poseidon," Ares said to Phorcys and Keto.

"They were attacked?" Keto asked with an expression that was far from surprised.

"Do you swear you had nothing to do with it?" Ares asked.

"We do not swear in this house." Phorcys whipped his fish tail down and stirred the waters around them. His pincer-like forelegs clacked opened and closed, opened and closed.

In a voice laced with threat, Ares said, "If you and your wife refuse to swear, we have no choice but to assume you're involved."

"As you wish," Phorcys said. "But we have no more to say, so you can either depart amicably, or I'll have to call Scylla and her sisters to help you on your way."

"Don't threaten me!" Ares stood up and puffed out his chest.

Than did the same, but inside, he felt helpless. Something had happened to Therese, and these two before him could be responsible. He narrowed his eyes, trying to read their faces.

"Be assured we will return," Ares added. "And you won't have known a sorrier day."

"How *is* Scylla these days?" Than finally asked, his heart rate increasing. "I wouldn't mind seeing her again."

Phorcys frowned. "She's busy at the moment."

Taking this for evidence, and no longer able to stand there without doing anything, Than multiplied into the fifties and bound the old man and his wife to their thrones. "I thought I smelled a bluff. What have you done with Therese?"

This is not the time! Ares prayed. *We're on their turf without reinforcements.*

I'm our reinforcements. Than multiplied into the dozens, ready to defend himself and Ares from attack. He was surprised the god of war wasn't more enthusiastic, and this chipped away a little of Than's confidence. He might not be doing the right thing, but he had to do something.

Then a long serpent's tail wrapped itself around Than's neck and threatened to snap off his head, debilitating the entire group of him.

Echidna.

Ares drew his sword and swung at the half-woman, half-serpent.

The serpent goddess hissed, and from her beautiful, humanoid face, a forked tongue flicked out and wrapped itself around the hilt of Ares's sword. Phorcys leaped forward and held Ares's boots with his pincers, demobilizing him. Keto reinforced the trap by wrapping her arms around the god of war's waist.

"Mmm," Keto said. "I've always wanted to kiss you, Ares."

"Stop that nonsense," Phorcys commanded.

Miles away in the Aegean, in the foyer of Poseidon's palace, Thanatos stared at the lord of the sea with wide eyes. His face went pale and he could barely breathe.

"What is it, my boy?" Poseidon asked with alarm.

Thanatos automatically reintegrated into one prisoner: The prisoner of Echidna.

***

Jen sat across the breakfast table from her mother and brother at the crack of dawn, dressed and ready to go to work in the barn. Neither her mom nor her brother had said a word about their trip to Tartarus, and Jen was beginning to fear it had all been a dream.

Had her brother and mother really witnessed Pete drinking Jen's blood?

She shuddered as she stirred some sugar and milk into her coffee. "Y'all doin' okay this morning?"

Bobby let out a deep breath. "I still can't believe it."

Their mother's eyes flooded with tears as she sipped at her coffee and sucked at a cigarette.

"Mom?" Jen asked.

"I don't know whether I'm pleased as punch or ready for the looney bin," her mother said.

A gentle knock at the door disturbed their conversation.

Bobby went to the front window. "It's Mr. Stern."

Jen met her mother's eyes and was surprised to see them crinkle into a smile. "Ain't no way in hell we're telling him about this. Y'all hear?"

Jen and Bobby grinned and nodded.

"Promise?" Mrs. Holt asked.

"Promise," they each said.

"My oldest son is in the Underworld and is fixin' to marry a Fury," Mrs. Holt muttered. "No, I just don't think John would take that very well."

All three of them giggled.

"Go ahead and let him in, Bobby," their mother said.

Jen was surprised at how well her mother received Mr. Stern when just a few days ago, she'd been begging him to leave.

"I'm sorry to bother you all," he said from the doorway.

Mrs. Holt went to the door. "Come on in, John. I'm glad to see you."

"You are?" His bushy eyebrows shot up in surprise.

"'Course." Mrs. Holt put out her cigarette and winked at Jen. "Don't say a word," she mouthed.

Jen smiled.

Mr. Stern stayed all morning to help with the chores. Jen could tell he enjoyed horse work and had a talent for it. Despite her own sadness over losing Hypnos to the evil Sith lord, Jen was overjoyed that her mother appeared to be happy.

But all morning long, she couldn't stop thinking about what Pete might have seen in her future that had made him go berserk. Did he see her with Hip? Is that what had made no sense?

As they returned to the house for lunch, Jen passed by the broken remnants of the dream globe and picked up one of the larger pieces. It glittered in the sunlight, felt like glass to the touch, but was cold, like ice. She closed her eyes and asked to see Hip. When nothing happened, as she had expected, she dropped the broken piece in the dirt, kicked it with her boot, and headed to the house. She washed up in her room, put on fresh clothes, and then picked up the crown from her side table. Now that her mother was feeling better, maybe it was time for Jen to be invisible again.

***

Hypnos flew across the Ionian Sea, where he had last sensed Therese. What could she be doing out this way? And why wasn't she answering him?

He settled on a rock on the Sicilian side of the Messina Straight and rested his chin in his hands. He needed to give up on his dream of finding a way to make Jen a goddess. It wasn't going to happen; instead, he needed to convince her that he was capable of loving her for the rest of her life—no matter how old and gray she lived to become.

But would she believe him? He doubted it. Mortals tended to be as vain as the gods and even more insecure.

He had gone centuries without love, so why did he need it now? He realized it wasn't love he needed; it was Jen. Her beautiful smile and fun-loving spirit and dedication to her family and friends warmed his heart. And the way she looked at him, kissed him, held him, wanted him—all those things filled him with joy and made him want to sing.

He covered his face with his hands and wept, hoping none of the gods could see.

At that moment Scylla burst from the water and gazed down at him with her six ugly heads. He'd forgotten the sheer expanse of her size and the innumerable rows of her teeth.

He unsheathed his sword and was about to go for one of the necks when he heard Therese's voice.

"Don't! It's me! It's Therese!"

Hip stared up at what he now realized was a docile monster, but that wasn't enough to convince him.

"Why would you say such a thing?" He pointed his sword toward Scylla.

"Because it's true!" the monster shrieked. "Ask me anything…about Jen, Pete, Mrs. Holt. Ask me about my twins!"

Hip thought for a minute. This was crazy, but okay. He'd play. "Which of the five challenges given by Hades did Therese fail?"

"I looked back!" the monster screeched. "I saw Than and forgot about everything else."

Still not convinced, Hip asked, "Where are Therese's parents?"

"They live on an elm tree in Colorado outside my house! They're Cardinals. I gave them immortality after Than helped me transfer their souls. Hip, it's me!" the monster raged.

Hip struggled to think of a question no one else would know the answer to.

"What animal did you change me into today and why?" he demanded.

"An ass, because you were being one! And you're being one now, Hip! Please help me!"

Hip staggered back. "How…"

"Circe did this to me."

"Why?"

"I don't know. She changed Scylla into a beautiful maiden and left me to take her place."

"What about the twins?" Hip asked, afraid of the answer.

"I still feel them, but I'm not sure." All six heads drooped toward the shore. "You've got to help me. I can't pray in this condition. Please find Than!"

Hip called to his brother and was shaken by Than's reply.

"How can this be happening?" Hip muttered.

"What?" Therese shrieked. "Has something happened to Than?"

The duties of Death called to him, and he disintegrated in time to join Poseidon in an attack against the Old Man of the Sea. Poseidon freed Ares by slicing through Echidna's tongue and hurling Phorcys across the room. Hip stabbed Echidna's serpent tail again and again until she loosened her grip on his brother. The duties of Death left Hypnos back to his own duties of Sleep. Phorcys and his family disappeared.

Than said, "We need to help Therese! She's been captured!"

"First we search the castle," Poseidon commanded. "We'll be more powerful with the aid of my trident."

Hip and Than helped the other Olympians search, but they found no sign of Amphitrite and the trident.

83

"Where could they be?" Poseidon said. "And who could be working with Phorcys?"

Hip scratched his chin. "Perhaps Circe."

"Circe? Why do you suspect her?" Ares asked.

Hip looked through the water at his brother, afraid to break his heart. "She's done something terrible."

Than's eyes widened. "Where's Therese?"

Chapter Seven: The Oldest Castle

Therese grabbed Hip in one claw, lifted him a foot off the ground, and screeched, "For the tenth time, tell me what's going on! Answer me!"

Before Hip could reply, Than appeared at her side, followed by Ares and Poseidon.

"Scylla!" Poseidon shouted.

"Not Scylla," Hip said. "Therese."

"How? And where's the real Scylla?" Ares asked.

"Circe changed her into a beautiful maiden," Hip explained. "We don't know where she is."

Therese was heartbroken by the sight of her husband's mortification. He frowned, squinted, and turned pale. This gave her a taste of how Scylla must have felt being looked upon for centuries with eyes of fear and disgust. No wonder Scylla had become cruel. The humiliation and the rejection were overwhelming.

Not to mention the awkward feeling of being in such a strange body. Her six necks were long and heavy to hold up, so they drooped in the middle, nearly touching the rocky beach. Her tentacles were difficult to control—almost as hard as it is for people to move their ears. In the water, she managed, though not without difficulty, but on land, it took all her energy not to fall over. The six dog-heads at her waist moved constantly, but not through her own volition. These canine parts yapped like an uncontrollable twitch.

"Than, it's me." Therese gently set Hip back on the rocky coast, but her feelings of insecurity couldn't prevent her words from sounding scratchy and harsh in the body of the monster. She was twice the size of the others, but she felt small and helpless.

"Therese?" Than asked with a look of incredulity that brought tears to Therese's four eyes.

"Help me," she cried.

"How do we know this isn't a trap?" Ares shouted.

"It's no trap," Hip said.

"Oh no." Than reached out and touched Therese's slimy arm. "Are you okay? Are the babies…"

She pulled her six heads close together and covered them with her claws. "I don't know. I think I feel them there, but this body is so…different. The dog-heads at my waist seem to have minds of their own."

All six dog-heads growled.

"Hera or Artemis can tell us," Poseidon suggested.

"Therese is more helpful to us in *this* form," Ares said. "We can send her as a spy…"

"No," Than said. "Absolutely not."

"You mean you didn't find Amphitrite with Phorcys and Keto?" Therese asked.

Ares recounted the story of what had happened. Then he added, "Zeus would forget about your act of treason against him if you helped us find the trident."

"Ares makes a good point," Poseidon said.

"No!" Than shouted. "Enough! We're going to Circe right now!"

"Your wife is not our priority," Ares said. "Finding the trident is."

"In the wrong hands, my trident could bring down Mount Olympus," Poseidon added. "Especially if there are more lightning bolts at large."

Therese unleashed an earth-shaking wail. "I need to know if I'm still carrying my babies!" she cried. Then in a lower, though still scratchy, voice she added, "If they're unharmed, and if you swear on the River Styx to do everything you can to change me back, I'll do whatever you want."

Than flew up and took one of her center heads in his hands. She was surprised by his gentle touch. He stroked her, and this show of affection in spite of her repulsive appearance made the tears flow from her eyes like rain.

"Oh, Than!"

He lifted one of her center heads, wiped away the tears, gazed in the one eye, and pleaded, "Don't do this. Let's go to Circe now."

"She uses black magic that makes her as powerful as any god," Therese screeched, hating her monstrous voice. "With their help," she pointed to the three other gods with one of her claws, "our chances improve."

"But what if the real Scylla has already told her parents?" Hip asked.

"She wouldn't," Poseidon said. "Circe transformed her once before, and Keto rejected Scylla and was outraged that she wanted to change her natural form. I highly doubt she would suffer the same rejection from her mother again."

"But we don't know for sure," Than said. "Let me go and scout it out. My duties take me near the castle all the time. In fact, I'm there now, and I can see the old man and his wife dining with Echidna."

"Licking their wounds. No doubt," Ares scoffed.

"No sign of Scylla?" Poseidon asked.

"Wait," Than said. "I see a girl hovering outside the castle. She has black hair, pale skin, and turquoise eyes."

"That's her!" Therese screeched.

"Damn!" Poseidon shouted. "I was sure…"

"Wait!" Than said. "She's looking at her parents through a window."

"Why?" Hip asked.

"I don't know. I can't tell for sure, because we're underwater, but I think she's crying."

"She must feel conflicted about her improved form," Poseidon speculated. "She has to choose between beauty and her mother's acceptance."

"It's so unfair," Therese screeched.

Hip shook his head. "You feel sorry for *her*?"

"She's such a bleeding heart," Ares complained. "She swims with baby penguins, for heaven's sake."

"I'll watch to be sure she doesn't stay," Than said, ignoring Ares's remark.

After several long minutes, Than finally said, "Poseidon was right. She doesn't want to face her mother. She's swimming away."

"Can you stay there and watch my back?" Therese filled with fear at the realization that she was about to go down into a house of monsters alone.

"I won't leave without you," her husband promised.

"I'll hide nearby, too," Hip said. "If things get out of control, I can put Phorcys and his household into the deep boon of sleep."

"Why don't we do that to begin with?" Therese asked.

"Because we need information," Ares said. "We've already searched the castle."

"I won't let anything bad happen to you," Poseidon said.

"Something bad already has," Therese moaned.

"Just find out all you can," Ares said.

"First call Artemis to make sure the babies are okay." Than pointed a finger at Ares. "That was part of the deal."

"I'm searching for her now," Hip said. "I left as soon as the idea was mentioned."

Than clamped a hand on his brother's shoulder. "You've always had my back."

"And I always will, bro'."

Artemis appeared with an arrow fitted to her bow. "Is this a trap?"

Therese rolled all four of her eyes and shook her heads in frustration. "It's not, Artemis. It's really me. Therese. Can you sense if I'm still carrying my babies?" That's all that really mattered to Therese: She needed to know her babies were okay.

Artemis returned her arrow to her quiver. "So help me, Hypnos, if this isn't Therese, I'll never help you again."

Ares laughed, and Than gave him a dirty look.

Artemis extended her palms out toward Therese and closed her eyes. Therese filled with anxiety and prayed to every god she knew to let her babies be okay. She didn't know if anyone could hear her, since she could no longer hear the prayers of others. Perhaps this monstrous body was incapable of prayer. But she prayed anyway.

Please let my babies be okay.

***

Than held his breath as he waited for Artemis to reply. He prayed to her to do everything in her power to save the twins. He prayed to Hera, and to Hestia, and to his mother, and to Aphrodite. He begged them all to come to his aid and save his children.

90

He was struck with emotion when they each appeared at his side. They listened to his explanations through prayer. Aphrodite, Hera, Hestia, Demeter, Persephone, and Hecate had all come. Soon after, Athena and her mother joined them. These goddesses, who often bickered among themselves, held hands in a ring around the body of Scylla and waited for Artemis's answer.

Hera lifted her chin, "I sense them."

"As do I!" Artemis said. "But wait."

"They're alive?" Therese screeched.

"They are crabs now," Hera said. "In eggs that want to be laid."

"Crabs?" Than repeated, his stomach sick.

"Don't lay them," Artemis added. "If you do, we might not be able to change them back."

Than felt faint. "Are they in danger?"

"As long as Therese resists the urge to lay them, the babies have a chance of becoming human again," Artemis said.

"And if she lays them?" Hip asked.

Artemis frowned. "They'll be born as crabs."

"But I can transform them," Therese shrieked. "We both can."

"We don't want your twins to start off as crabs," Artemis said. "Even if we change them, they'll never be like real humans."

"Just don't lay the eggs," Hera said. "No matter how great the pressure becomes. And the pressure will become great."

"How long before that happens?" Than asked as he raked a shaky hand through his hair.

"I don't know," Hera said.

"Will you come with us to Circe's lair?" Than asked the goddesses.

"First Therese must spy on Phorcys," Ares objected.

"There may be no time," Than said.

Poseidon lifted a finger into the air. "Recovering the trident must be our priority."

"But our twins are destined to restore faith to humanity," Than argued. "They should be a priority, too."

"And they will be," Poseidon assured him. "But we need the trident first, or there might not be a Mount Olympus in which to restore people's faith."

All eyes turned to Therese. Than's heart filled with dread.

"Since I don't feel any pressure yet, I'll do it," Therese said. "But all of you must swear on the River Styx that you'll help me when I return."

Everyone swore, including Than, though he felt too sick to utter it aloud.

***

Following the instructions from Ares and Poseidon, Therese swam down into the depths of the Ionian Sea toward the most ancient castle in existence. The monstrous body was awkward to maneuver through the water. Therese tried all the strokes she knew, but none of them worked well, so she ended up paddling like a dog with her claws and shaking her tentacles in something like a dolphin kick. It didn't help that she was nervous and trembling. The six long necks slowed her down until she figured out how to hold them together in front of her. The dogs at her waist yapped with a will of their own and continued to feel like involuntary muscles that twitched of their own accord.

When she reached the door to the castle, she prayed to Than, *Do I knock or just walk inside?*

Than didn't answer. Then she remembered that she was without the ability to communicate through prayer in this monstrous body. Her heart—if this body had one—seemed to skip a beat.

Whenever she went to visit her aunt and uncle, she always knocked and walked inside, without waiting for anyone to answer. She decided to use this same approach at the castle door.

She knocked. "It's Scylla." Then she entered.

There were two huge crawfish standing guard in the foyer, but they made no move to prevent her passing.

Phorcys and Keto sat opposite one another at the ends of a long banquet table. Echidna sat in the middle. Although the table was long and they were far apart, this gave their tails ample room. Phorcys and Keto's fish tails were covered with iridescent scales. Echidna's serpent tail had a snake head at the end. Echidna's face, like Keto's, was beautiful, but the darting tongues from both ends of her body were creepy-looking.

Of course, who am I to call someone creepy-looking? Therese thought.

From another room, the Chimera, entered, sending a shiver down all six of Therese's necks. "Hello, Scylla."

"Hello." Therese maneuvered to the table, where platters of oysters were spread from end to end, and she sat beside the three-headed Chimera.

The Chimera's front head and body looked like a lioness, but in place of a tail, there was the head of a fire-breathing snake. From the lion's back sprang a goat's head.

"What evil work did Circe make you do for her today?" Chimera spoke from the head of the goat as the lion's head slurped up the flesh from the oyster shell.

As Therese struggled to come up with an answer, it was apparent to her at this close proximity that Scylla had, by far, the worst body of them all. "She had me distract the gods who came to pay you a visit."

"Why?" Phorcys asked. In addition to a tail, two crawfish pinchers grew from his waist, which clicked and clacked as he spoke.

Therese shivered. "I don't know. I guess she didn't want them snooping around your castle walls."

"But she knows they won't find anything here," Keto said. "That makes no sense."

The monsters' eyes turned on Therese. She fought the panic threatening to tighten all six throats. "Maybe she thought they might try another attack."

"Those Olympians should know we aren't stupid enough to keep Amphitrite here," Phorcys said.

"They care more about the trident," Keto said.

"I can't wait until it's mine." Phorcys laughed haughtily. "It's the only reason I'm putting up with this whole business."

"Do you think the Olympians will figure out where the trident and Amphitrite have been hidden?" Therese asked.

"Never!" the Chimera screeched. "No one would ever guess."

"As long as everyone in this family remains loyal to the Titans, the Olympians will fall," Phorcys said.

"That's the catch, isn't it?" Echidna said. "And our weakest link is sitting on the trident."

"What do you mean?" Therese asked.

"Don't be an idiot," the Chimera said to Therese. "You know what Echidna says is true. We all know it."

"Ask Charbydis to come tomorrow," Phorcys said to Therese. "I have something I need to say to her."

"Aren't you going to feed?" Echidna asked her.

"I'm not hungry," Therese said.

"There's a first." The Chimera laughed. "Are you ill?"

"You certainly are acting strange today, Scylla," Keto commented. "Is there something you aren't telling us?"

"No!" Therese shrieked, ready to run.

"Circe had no message for me?" Phorcys asked.

"None," Therese replied.

"If you aren't going to eat with us, then why did you come?" Keto asked.

Without a word, Therese swam from the castle doors as fast as she could manage.

     ***

Hypnos sighed with relief when they had all returned safely to Mount Olympus where they conveyed to the other gods what had transpired.

Zeus struck his fist into a palm and said, "Attacking Circe will get us nowhere."

Hip glanced at his brother, whose face had gone pale.

"But these gods swore to help us," Than said.

"We swore an oath," Hip clarified.

"And so you shall help, Hypnos," Zeus said.

"What do you have in mind?" Hades suddenly appeared. "I've been tied up below, but I get the gist of things. Therese needs Circe to transform her, and all the gods swore to help." Then, to Therese's dog-heads, he added, "Down boys."

"We need to interrogate Cerberus," Poseidon said.

"And also Orthrus, Ladon, Charbydis, the Hydra, and the other children of Keto," Artemis put in.

"Before you upset Cerberus, find the spy in your own house," Hades said to Poseidon.

Than stood at their center and spun in a circle, eyeing each one of the gods. "You all swore to help Therese as soon as she returned from the ancient castle."

"Hypnos is our best bet of winning Circe's favor," Zeus said. "We could overtake her, but she can't be forced to act against her will. She loves no one; not even herself."

"What can I do?" Hip was eager to help his brother and Therese.

"Make her fall in love with you," Zeus said. "Once she loves you, she will do anything for you."

Hip rubbed his chin, a gesture he picked up from his father, and it made him feel foolish because he had no beard.

Zeus continued, "You are the only god among us whose heart yet belongs to no one."

Whether they were loyal or not, all of the other gods had a wife except for Apollo and Hermes. Everyone knew Apollo's heart had been claimed in recent years by a mortal, but what of Hermes? Hypnos studied him and was suddenly aware by the look in Hermes's eyes as they gazed across the room at Hecate, and also by the look she returned him, that his heart belonged to someone, too.

Hip's heart belonged to someone, but no one here, except for his brother and Therese, cared one bit about it. Than and Therese were his very best friends, and if this is what it took to help them, he would do it.

"I'll go," Hip said.

Chapter Eight: Circe's Lair

Hypnos had been both surprised and relieved when his cousin Hermes had volunteered to go with him to Circe's Island. He was grateful to have him by his side as they flew across the Ionian Sea. Unaware of their mission, Circe's father and his cup dipped far in the west, spreading golden hues across the surface of the sea. Hip hoped to reach the witch's house before nightfall, because that's when she was known to scream.

"Follow me," Hermes said, once they had landed on the rocky shore.

They headed toward the center of the island on foot, because to god travel would make them vulnerable to dark magic, and because they needed to find a certain herb before reaching the witch's lair. They soon became consumed by a thick forest, which blocked most of the light left from Helios; but, being gods, they could see in the dark, and so they trod on.

Hermes led them up a steep hill where they were once again bathed with the light of the setting sun. From this point, they could see the entire island. At its center, transparent smoke ascended in puffs, like the steam from an engine. Hypnos had never seen smoke so clear before.

"That's strange," he said to Hermes.

"Her potions and herbs," Hermes explained. "Wretched stuff. Try not to breathe it in."

That sounded easy, considering the fact that he had no power to choose the air he breathed.

Hermes set about searching the top of the hill for the plant they needed to serve as an antidote to Circe's brew, the one she used on Odysseus and his men, and countless others before and since.

"What does this plant look like?" Hip asked, wishing he weren't utterly useless.

"Ah, here it is." Hermes plucked a white flower from the ground. "Moly."

From its black roots, clumps of dirt clung.

"It's a powerful herb and doesn't come up easily," Hermes added. "Only gods can pluck it. See how the dirt refuses to release it?"

"Hmm." Everything about this place was freaky.

Hermes used his fingers to carefully clean the black root of dirt. Then Hypnos followed his cousin down the hill toward the center of the island and the poisonous puffs of smoke.

Despite his fear over meeting with the witch, the hike through the woods invigorated Hip. His job rarely afforded him opportunities like this. As they trod on, he began to fantasize about hiking with Jen through the woods behind her house, about finding a cool spot near the stream and lying down on the soft dirt, and…

Soon they reached a clearing, and Circe's house came into view. It was made of cut stone, polished to a sheen, which, even in the fading light, sparkled. It was angular, like a modern city complex, capturing the light and reflecting it back in all directions. From a triangular chimney, the clear smoke ascended in clouds much larger than they had appeared from a distance. Surrounding the house were six wolves and six mountain lions. Three of them slept, but the rest paced nervously, like caged animals, though no fence penned them in.

"Don't worry," Hermes whispered. "The animals are friendly."

"You could have fooled me."

"Circe has used her magic to turn them into pets."

"What is her deal?" Hypnos asked. "Why does she live as a witch using black magic when she's a goddess?"

"She's a Titaness," Hermes explained.

"So? I know several, and they aren't witches. Hecate, for example."

Hypnos realized immediately by Hermes's expression that he had hit a sensitive cord.

"She's your mother's slave," Hermes muttered.

"Not slave. Companion." Hypnos felt offended on his mother's behalf. "My mom's not like that."

Hermes gave no reply.

Hypnos didn't like this change in subject. "So, back to Circe."

"Her father dropped her on this island when she was very young and left her here to fend for herself. Her mother didn't want her, either. So, this is what she came up with."

"The life of a lonely witch," Hip muttered. "Do you think she's the one who stole the trident and abducted Amphitrite?"

"That's for her to know and for you to find out, cousin."

***

Than stroked one of Therese's six necks as she bathed in Poseidon's enormous spa on Mount Olympus. He was grateful the Olympians had allowed her to stay here in the strongest fortress on earth, where many gods could be at hand if the pressure to lay the eggs containing their twins became too great. But he was worried about his brother.

"Poor Hip," she said, as if reading his mind.

He gave her a weak smile. "He'll be fine."

"Don't look at me," Therese said again, covering her four eyes with her claws. "Look at the wall or the floor. I can't stand for you to see me like this."

"I'm telling you, I *don't* see you like this," he insisted gently. "When I look at you, I see the real you. And anyway, it wouldn't matter if you were stuck in this body forever. I love you."

Evidently, he had said the wrong thing. *Again.*

Through tears that sloshed into the spa and made the soaking water turbulent, Therese said, "Forever? Oh, gods, I hope not."

"I won't let that happen," Than said.

Therese dropped her claws to her sides and closed all four eyes. "I know I'm being ridiculous."

"Not at all. It can't be easy."

"You're so good to me. Maybe it's hormones."

That made Than laugh. He stroked her arms and necks—avoiding the six dog-heads.

"I'm going to stop feeling sorry for myself right now, and I'm going to do what I can to help find Amphitrite and the trident," she said.

"Just be patient and have faith. Keto's children are all being interrogated, thanks to you. You've done enough."

"I can't just lie here," she screeched.

He missed her sweet voice. "What else is there for you to do?"

She sat up in the tub, splashing water all over him. "Oops."

"It's just water." He found a towel and dried himself.

"I'm going to see Polyphemus," she said.

His mouth dropped open. "No, Therese."

"Poseidon said it felt like a lightning bolt. It *had* to come from his sheep."

"Yes, but…"

103

"Maybe if I can find out who stole the trident and abducted Amphitrite, it will give me the leverage I need to convince Zeus and the others to give Melinoe a shot at redemption."

"But you're in no condition…"

"I'm in perfect condition." She raised her pincers above her head. "This is the absolute best condition for talking to a ferocious cannibal. Are you coming with me, or not?"

***

Hermes handed the plant over to Hypnos, "Eat all of it. The flower and the root."

Hip brushed a little more of the dirt from the herb and sniffed it. "What's this thing supposed to do again?"

As Hermes spoke, Hip kept his eyes on the witch, visible now through two front open windows. A tapestry hung along the back wall, and she appeared to be weaving it.

Hermes said, "She's going to mix up a concoction for you to drink."

"A concoction?"

"Yeah. Made of her potions and animal bones and what not."

"Sounds disgusting."

"Everyone, including Odysseus, says it's delicious, unlike that plant you're about to eat."

"Great."

"But if you don't eat the plant, her concoction will turn you into a pig."

"A literal pig?"

"That's right. And then she'll eat you."

Hip rubbed his chin. "You sure this flower will protect me?"

"Positive."

Hypnos plucked a white petal and ate it. So far so good. When there were no more petals left, he ate the stem. Awful, but tolerable. Then he took a bite of the black root. Oh, hell. The skin of the root tasted like tar, and the juice inside reminded him of human blood—bitter and metallic and nasty. He wasn't sure he'd be able to keep it down. He wrinkled his nose and chewed quickly.

"Now, there's something else you need to know," Hermes said.

Hip looked up at him through squinted eyes. He swallowed down the last bite.

"Circe will wave a wand over you as you finish the concoction."

"A wand? Seriously?"

"It's a stick from a willow tree, I think. Enchanted, of course."

"Of course."

"As soon as she pulls out that wand, draw your sword and rush at her, like you mean to kill her."

"But why would I do that? She's immortal."

"Just do it, okay?"

"Okay. Whatever you say."

"Now, here's the worst part—or the best, depending on your outlook."

"Will you just spit it out?" Hip wanted to get this over with.

"She'll be frightened by your sword and will invite you to her bed."

Hip's eyebrows shot up. "Huh? I don't think so."

"You have to go to bed with her. Any man who gets that far wins her trust and love."

"No one said anything about sleeping with her." Hip thought of Jen.

"It's just sleeping," Hermes said. "She'll be frightened and want you in bed with her for protection. Just kiss her and stroke her hair until she falls asleep."

Hypnos did not like the way this was going. Maybe he could put Circe in the deep boon of sleep before he had to kiss her.

"And don't make her fall asleep before she's had a chance to fall in love with you," Hermes added.

"Oh, crap."

"Because that's when she'll start talking. As soon as she feels romantic toward you, you can ask her if she knows anything about the trident."

"And what about Therese?"

"Well, you'll want to ask the witch to change her back, obviously."

"Obviously."

"Go before night falls." Hermes slapped Hip's back affectionately. "And good luck."

Hip picked his way through the woods and into the witch's clearing with a sense of doom. The dogs and mountain lions noticed him immediately and rushed toward him. As Hermes had said, they were friendly. They each took a turn lifting their front paws and falling against Hip's knees to be patted on the head or scratched behind the ears. Far from being a nuisance, these actions brought Hip a bit of comfort as he made his way to Circe's door.

She opened it before he could knock. He was stunned by her bright golden hair, which fell in tight ropes down her shoulders and arms. When he met her eyes, he found they were the same color gold as her hair, and they emitted soft light, like a bedside lamp. Her ruby lips, by contrast, were dark, and before he could look away, they spread into a seductive grin.

"Come to bring me sweet dreams in the flesh?"

He stuffed his hands in his front trouser pockets and grinned sheepishly. "Um, something like that."

"You're too cute."

"Um, thank you?" He scratched his head, not sure what to do with his hands.

She arched a brow. "Do you start all your sentences with 'um'?"

"Um, no." He laughed and was relieved when she did, too. "May I come in?"

He was appalled, at first, as he followed her inside and took a look around, by the jars of various animal parts, insects, and plants on display on her shelves. A bubbling cauldron sat on a grate over the fire—the source of the clear and poisonous smoke.

Despite all of these ghastly things, the light from Circe's hair and eyes exceeded the glow from his body, and it reflected on the amazing architecture of the polished stone, creating a beautiful haze, like soft sunlight breaking through a clearing in a forest.

"Nice place," he said.

"I'm glad you approve. Please, have a seat." She motioned to the white chairs before the bubbling cauldron. "I'll get you something to drink. It's my own special formula."

He watched her ladle the brew from the bubbling cauldron into a golden cup. As she handed it to him, she asked, "Would you care for something to eat? I have some fresh ham from a pig I slaughtered this morning."

Hypnos wondered if the pig had once been an unfortunate visitor, but he dared not refuse. "If you'll join me, I'd love to."

He waited to drink the brew until she was seated in the chair beside his with a plate of sliced ham, which she sat on a glass table between them. Hermes had been right. The brew was delicious.

"Mmm. This is good," he said.

She gave him an expectant smile. He drank the cup down to the last drop and set it next to the ham. Circe frowned.

"Is something wrong?" he asked, trying not to gloat.

She brought out a crooked wand from beneath her white silk gown. Hip drew his sword and pointed the blade at her neck.

Circe laughed. "You do know I'm immortal."

This wasn't how Hermes had said she would react.

"What do you intend to do with that wand?" he asked.

She flicked it. Across the room, on one of the many shelves, a set of wooden marionettes came to life and danced to music.

"Is that so bad?" she asked.

He sheathed the sword. "My apologies." So much for inviting him to her bed. He let out a breath of relief.

She returned her wand to a pocket inside her gown. "I like to have the puppets dancing when the sun goes down. They distract me from the blood."

"Blood?" His voice cracked.

"At night it pours down the walls inside this house and frightens me. I suppose it's my sins. They come to mock me." She glanced around the room. "Ah. Here it comes."

Hip saw no blood. The witch was mad.

"So that's why I sometimes hear you scream?" he asked carefully.

"All night long, the blood flows and fills my house. It's the blood of every animal I have slaughtered for my spells and curses. We'll have to run to my woods before too long, or we'll drown."

"You sleep in the woods each night?"

"Not sleep. I never sleep."

"But even gods need to sleep *some* time."

"Believe me, I know. But the blood…it…"

"Circe, I don't see it."

She glared at him.

"I can help you," he added. "Remember who I am?"

"I know why you're here. Why should I trust you?"

"We can make a deal."

She stood up and wrapped her arms around herself. "That herb Hermes gave you to eat won't protect you from everything. Did you know that?"

He stood now, too. "A deal that's good for the both of us."

"I won't tell you where the trident is, Hypnos."

"I don't care about the trident." This wasn't exactly a lie. "I only care about my brother."

She looked hard at him for several long seconds. He held his breath.

"Fine." She stepped closer to him, closing the distance between them. "Stay here with me tonight. Give me one night of peaceful dreams. In the morning, I'll return your brother's wife to her natural form."

He searched her bright eyes for some sign of foul play. He needed to word the oath carefully, to avoid a trap. What if this witch made Therese a mortal? That was, after all, her "natural form."

"Swear, on the River Styx, that, if I give you one night's rest, Therese will return to her normal form as the goddess of animal companions. And swear that her babies will return to normal, too, unharmed."

The corners of her mouth twitched into a wry smile. "I swear."

Chapter Nine: Tricks and Tribulations

Therese flew in Scylla's clunky body across the night sky with Thanatos. When they reached the Ionian Sea, they plunged into the dark water and swam down deep to the caverns beneath Cyclopes Island. They made their way through a maze of tunnels until they came to the sink hole in Polyphemus's cave. Than hid beneath the surface as Therese popped up and frightened the sleeping cannibal and his few remaining sheep.

"Scylla?" the giant sat up, rubbed his one eye, blinked, and looked blankly at Therese. "Why have you come to wake me in the night? Haven't I sacrificed enough already?"

"What have you sacrificed?" Therese said in Scylla's scratchy voice.

Tears flowed from the cannibal's eyes. "Yer heart is even crueler than my mother's. I *loved* them sheep!"

"Your mother?" Therese asked, not sure who his mother even was. Was it Amphitrite? Therese wished she could pray to Than to find out.

"Don't you and yer sister speak? She's the one who came and took em and gave em to Atlas. Just tell me why yer here and get on wit it!"

A basket of eggs appeared on the ground near Polyphemus's bed. Than must have done it.

Polyphemus's face lit up with a smile that cracked his face in half. "Yer brought me breakfast? Why?" Without getting up, he transferred some of the eggs into the pot hanging over a fire.

Therese came up with a plan. "Someone cursed my memory. I need your help."

Polyphemus frowned.

"I forgot where we hid Amphitrite and the trident," Therese said.

The Cyclops climbed to his feet just as Helios began to rise in the east and sprinkle the cave with a few bright rays. "You better leave my sight right now, if you had anything to do wit it!" Polyphemus roared. "I told my mother I wanted no part of Atlas's treachery!"

"Why haven't you told Poseidon?" Therese screeched in Scylla's voice.

"My mother said Atlas would chop me up and eat me if I said a word."

Therese felt a tremendous pressure on her entire form, pressing from all directions. She was helpless to do anything about it. Certain Polyphemus had attacked her with some unknown magic, she screamed in Scylla's monstrous roar, closed all four eyes, and flailed frantically with her claws.

Moments after, she was startled when her screams began to sound like her own voice—a delusion of the magic, no doubt. She opened her eyes to see Polyphemus blinking dumbly at her.

The shock of being in her own body had no time to wear off before the cannibal had found his club and had raised it over his head.

"Why, you!" He swung the club.

She flew up to the ceiling, his wooden club grazing her foot. "I'm on your side!"

He swung at her again, like she was a baseball pitched too high.

"I'm on your father's side!" she said again. "I'm trying to help him!"

"Why should I believe you?" the Cyclops demanded.

Than appeared beside her and took her hand. "Let's go."

Together, they god traveled away from the island and headed back to Mount Olympus.

When they arrived outside the gates, Than asked, "You're okay? And the babies, too?"

She nodded, as tears of relief poured down her cheeks. She pressed her hands against her abdomen and felt Hestia and Hermes do the same. The sensation of their tiny baby hands held up to hers overwhelmed her with emotion. "The twins are fine."

She noticed him let out a big breath and close his eyes.

She clutched the lockets around her neck, thankful that they hadn't disappeared in the transformation.

"What a relief," he said.

In a hurry to share what they learned with the other gods, Therese gave the request to the Seasons to be allowed inside;

but, before she broached the gates, Than tugged at her hand and pulled her back into him. "Wait."

She used her thumbs to wipe a few tears from his cheeks. "What is it, honey? I'm okay. The babies are fine."

"I know we have to go in there and tell everyone what we've learned about Atlas, but for just one minute, let me hold my family."

Therese gladly nestled her face against his neck and drank in his smell. She enjoyed the feel of his hands along her body and in her hair. She took in the pleasure of running her hands through his thick, dark hair and tried not to think about the fact that once the twins were born, they'd never be a family again.

"Thank you," she whispered.

"The pleasure's always mine." He took her hand and led her through the courtyard.

As they ascended the rainbow steps, she asked, "Have you been in contact with Hip? Have you thanked him for me?"

"No. But look. There's Hermes. Maybe he has some news."

***

Jen set the crown on her bedside table and climbed beneath the bedcovers. Based on tonight's announcement, her mother and Mr. Stern were going to be married and live happily ever after. Pete was going to marry Tizzie and have his happily ever after, too—sort of. Yet never had Jen felt a bigger void inside her heart. Why couldn't she be grateful?

For the hundredth time, she wished she hadn't destroyed the dream globe. If only she could see Hip's face one more time. Maybe that would be enough. She closed her eyes but fought the urge to pray to him. He had moved on. He didn't want her anymore.

Sometime later, she was running through an empty field, like the one across from her house by the lake, but bigger, vaster, never-ending. She had to get to the end of it, so she ran on. She wasn't sure why she was running, or what it was she was running toward, but nevertheless she ran at her top speed.

Suddenly a giant body of water stretched out in front of her, dark and mysterious, but she had to keep going, so she did the only thing she could do and dived in. The taste of salt reminded her that this was not the lake in front of her house but a giant ocean of possibilities.

That's when he appeared before her.

"Why is it always the sea?" he asked. "I'm a land lover." He took her hand. "Shall we?"

Now they were in the woods behind her house hiking up the mountain along the stream. Hip led the way, her hand in his. He smiled back at her.

"Figment," she said.

She didn't want to give the command. She didn't care if he was a figment. She wanted to enjoy the dream.

He brought her to a clearing beside the stream, and they lay beside one another on a bed of warm leaves.

"I've missed you," he said.

She said nothing as he covered her mouth with his, and she was swept away, tears streaming down her cheeks, the void in her heart overwhelmed with love, the longing and tugging and bearing down of weight and cold and sorrow lifted up, high above them into the clouds.

She rejoiced and kissed him again and again and said, "Stay with me, oh please. Even if you are a figment. Stay with me."

He pulled her closer against him and whispered into her ear, "I'm no figment, Jen. It's me. Really me. And I love you and want to be with you for as long as you live."

Now the fear of deception ripped a hole where the void had been filled, and, like the air in a deflating balloon, the hopes and dreams and happiness flew out and away. As much as she relished the feel of him in her arms, kissing her, whispering his sweet nothings, she knew at some point she would have to wake up and know the truth. Might as well face it. Hell and damn. She grit her teeth, steeled herself for the hard slap of reality.

"Figment, I command you to show yourself."

He smiled back at her. "Believe me now?"

Her eyes and mouth widened. Could this be real? "Is this a dream from the gates of ivory or horn?" she murmured.

"Horn," he said. "It's a true dream, and I really do love you."

"What about Pa*shit*ea?"

He laughed, and when she frowned he apologized. "I'm laughing at your name for her, not at you. I was shot by the arrow of Eros. Zeus's command. Long story, darling, but it's you I want…"

She didn't wait for the rest of his explanation. She buried him with her kisses, praying to him to let this be the longest dream of her life.

***

Hypnos caressed Jen's soft hair—soft even in the world of dreams—and whispered against her ear, "I love you. I will always love you."

As he pressed his lips to hers, a burning pain, like a fire searing his flesh, shot through his skin. The fire travelled from his mouth to the ends of his fingertips and toes. He gasped and writhed in pain, and, when he opened his eyes, he saw Circe looking back at him, her head on his pillow, and her face inches from his, wearing a wry grin.

When the pain had at last subsided, Hip asked, "What just happened?"

She reached over and brushed his hair from his eyes and then planted a kiss on his cheek. Hip found it impossible to move away from her.

"I've restored your brother's wife and her twins as promised," Circe said gently.

Hip closed his eyes, sighed, and opened them again. "Thank you."

"I want to tell you something." She stroked his hair and looked intently into his eyes, as though he and Circe were lovers. "There are two kinds of men who visit me—and they're always men, never women. Sometimes travelers, sometimes explorers, sometimes wretched people who need something from me, and sometimes they're simply curious about me. Nevertheless, they all fall into two categories: swine or men."

Hip blinked at her, wondering what she was getting at.

"If they're swine, I turn them into their true form and keep them in my pigsty until I've fattened them up for slaughter. If they're men, I bring them to my bed and keep them until I grow weary of them."

"What do you mean you 'keep them'?"

"It's the only time I can sleep. When I have a warm body beside me."

Hip narrowed his eyes.

"And last night was the best sleep of all, thanks to you."

"Circe, I can come and give you nights like that as often as you'd like."

"I don't believe you."

Hip sat up in the bed and swung his feet to the floor, but when he tried to stand, he found he couldn't. An invisible force kept him on the bed. He turned and glared at the witch.

"What have you done?"

"Don't be cross." She gave him a playful smile.

***

Thanatos followed Therese up the rainbow steps and into the great hall of Mount Olympus. Hermes met them near the entrance with a grave look on his face.

"Where's Hip?" Than asked.

"Circe managed to get a spell past me," the messenger god replied.

"What?" Therese asked.

"I left the island to find *you*," Hermes said.

"But why?" Therese asked.

"To make sure the witch kept her word. To make sure she changed you back."

"Hermes, what spell?" Than asked. "What did Circe do to my brother?"

"She's trapped him in her bed."

Than disintegrated and god-travelled to Circe's Island, where he was about to multiply into the hundreds and converge upon the witch's house when Hermes grabbed him by the arm back on Mount Olympus.

"We need a plan," Hermes warned. "Don't just go in there willy nilly."

Than cocked his head to one side. "You and Hip had a plan."

"Therese!" Aphrodite cried from across the hall. "Look! Therese is back to her lovely self!"

Aphrodite and her Graces rushed to embrace Therese. Persephone, Hecate, and Demeter were right behind them. Pasithea avoided Than's eyes as she, too, welcomed Therese. Unlike the others, she wore a frown, which made Than feel sorry for her.

"Thank goodness!" Persephone said.

"Thank Hypnos," Than corrected.

Therese lifted her chin. "And now he needs our help."

"We know," Zeus called from his throne on the other side of the room. "Come in. We were just discussing what to do."

Athena, Metis, and Rhea stood near Zeus and Hera's double throne. Hephaestus was working in his forge, Hestia was busy preparing a meal, and both Poseidon and Hades were at their respective kingdoms. Ares, Apollo, and Artemis were not at home. They'd been sent to question gods and goddesses and other beings around the world.

"So why Cyclopes Island?" Hermes asked as they crossed into the great hall together.

"Therese had a hunch," Than said.

"Polyphemus knew who stole his sheep," Therese said.

The room grew deathly silent. Than gave Therese a reassuring wink. She squeezed his hand.

You're amazing, Than prayed to her.

You're *amazing*, she argued back.

"The Cyclops named the thief?" Zeus stood from his throne, and the women with whom he'd been consulting turned to face Therese, Than, and Hermes as they took the center of the room.

"He said his mother took them," Therese said.

"Thoosa?" Athena asked. "But why?"

"She's working for Atlas," Therese said. "Ares freed him, remember?"

"Hermes," Zeus began. "Ask Poseidon and Hades to come at once."

Hermes disappeared.

"What about my brother?" Than asked.

Metis and Athena exchanged worried looks.

"I'm sorry Thanatos." Rhea was the one who spoke. "You understand that getting back the trident must be our top priority, don't you?"

"We can split up," Than said.

"Not until we know more about Circe's involvement with Atlas and Thoosa," Zeus said. "Be patient, Thanatos."

Than told his father about Hip through prayer, expressing their urgent need to rescue him.

At that moment Poseidon entered the court dragging behind his golden net. The net contained a prisoner, who was curled in a ball like a giant fish. It was the merwoman called Thoosa, also known as the mother of Polyphemus.

Chapter Ten: Prisoners and Thieves

"Introducing my spy!" Poseidon shouted to the gods and goddesses surrounding his prisoner, just as Hades and Hermes entered the court.

Therese stepped closer to the golden net. Memories of being held prisoner in it flooded her. That's how she had come to Mount Olympus for the very first time. She couldn't help but feel a tinge of sympathy for the mermaid.

Thoosa was as beautiful as Keto and Echidna, if not more so. She shared their deep turquoise eyes and raven hair. It was hard to believe she and Poseidon had produced the giant, one-eyed cannibal known as Polyphemus. This proof that children don't always look like their parents made Therese clutch her belly.

"She refuses to tell me where she's hidden the trident!" Poseidon's eyebrows disappeared beneath his sun-bleached bangs. "Or Amphitrite, for that matter."

Therese noticed Amphitrite's abduction was always an afterthought, but she supposed more was at stake with the trident in the wrong hands.

"If you want to avoid our wrath, you'll speak!" Zeus commanded.

Thoosa flopped to her other side to face the lord of the gods. "I don't know where they are. I already told Poseidon, I had no idea they were stolen."

Therese narrowed her eyes, wanting to confront the sea nymph, but she held back.

"Did you or did you not give Polyphemus's sheep to Atlas?" Zeus asked.

"I did," Thoosa admitted. "But I didn't know he'd use them to take Amphitrite and the trident!"

Zeus turned to Hermes. "Bring Apollo home."

Hermes vanished.

"Make her swear an oath!" Poseidon said.

"I swear on the River Styx!" the mermaid cried. "Atlas wanted me to create a diversion for Poseidon, in case Polyphemus called his father while I was stealing the sheep." Thoosa covered her face and shook her head. "If only I'd known."

"What happened next?" Hera asked.

"I gave Amphitrite the idea of getting revenge on my sister, Scylla. Scylla deserved it."

"So you planted that idea in my wife's head?" Poseidon clenched his fists.

"I never imagined Atlas would attack my lord and lady. You must believe me!" Thoosa cried.

"Why do you think Atlas wanted those sheep?" Hades picked at his beard. "Lamb chops?"

"He said he loved me." Thoosa covered her face again. "He said he wanted to start a life together. A simple life in the sea. He said after centuries of standing on the earth and holding up the sky, he wanted nothing to do with those realms."

"Then what reason did he give you for wanting the sheep?" Hermes asked.

"He said he wanted to give them to his daughters, the Hesperides."

Hera stood from her throne. "Did he say why?"

"As a gift," Thoosa replied. "He said he hadn't been able to give them much over the years, and he thought they would enjoy having the wool, for making new clothes and such. It *is* the finest wool, after all."

"When was the last time you spoke to him?" Athena asked.

Thoosa shook her head and shrugged. "Not since the day I gave him the sheep."

Zeus lifted his fists in frustration. "Do you have any idea where he might be?"

"I didn't know your lightning bolts were hidden in those sheep. Please, believe me, Lord Zeus!"

Therese prayed to Than, *This isn't the first time one of Zeus's plans backfired on him.*

And us, Than replied with a grim look on his face.

Apollo and Artemis appeared with Hermes, and Apollo began to question the prisoner.

You okay? Therese put a hand on Than's shoulder, but dared not speak out loud.

I'm spying on Circe. I want to save Hip. He went there to help you and me.

I know. Therese frowned. *Please be careful. It won't do us any good if you get caught, too.*

Than squeezed her hand. *I can't communicate with him, but I can see him. He's trapped in her bed. He can't disintegrate.*

So, can he perform his duties?

No.

Then maybe now we can get some help.

Zeus will want mortals to have their sleep, Than agreed.

After Apollo finished questioning Thoosa, who was telling the truth, Than stuck his hand in the air and said, "Maybe Circe knows where Atlas is. I move we search her lair and question her."

The gods seemed to consider this.

"Mortals will not sleep as long as Hypnos is her prisoner," Hades added.

"Maybe we should use Thoosa to draw Atlas out," Poseidon said.

"His daughters are being interrogated by Ares in my garden now," Hera pointed out.

"Ares is the one responsible for freeing Atlas," Therese said again. "Shouldn't he be questioned?"

Therese noticed Than's face fall into a frown.

Should I not have said that? Therese asked Than.

It won't help us rescue Hip.

127

"I need volunteers to go to the Hesperides," Zeus said. "We'll get to the bottom of this."

As Apollo, Artemis, and others stepped forward to volunteer, Than took Therese's elbow and led her back to the rainbow steps.

"It looks like we're on our own for now," he said.

"What do you have in mind?" Therese asked.

"I want to take my father's helm."

"Can't you just ask to borrow it?"

Than shook his head. "I already did. He won't allow it. Not right now."

"But Hip's his son!"

"He says Circe is harmless."

Therese's mouth dropped open. "How can he say that after what she did to me? Our twins could have…" She couldn't finish—couldn't say it. She shuddered as she gently rubbed her abdomen, hoping the babies weren't advanced enough to know what had almost happened to them.

"My father says that she's taken Hip as her lover, and she treats her lovers well."

"Her lover?" Therese's stomach tied in knots. She hoped Jen would never find out.

"We have no choice but to take the helm," Than said. "The witch will sense me otherwise. I'll have it back before Hades even realizes it's gone."

128

"Why can't we wait until we have your father's approval?"

"Circe has a way of brainwashing her victims," Than explained. "We need to get Hip out of there while he still wants out."

Therese chewed on her bottom lip. She had to help. She had to. "What's your plan?"

Than bowed his head. "First, I'm going to kill my brother."

Therese held her breath and searched her husband's eyes. Had she heard him right?

"It's the only way to break her spell," he explained.

"So you're serious? You're going to kill him?"

Therese knew the only way to separate a god's body from his soul was to tear the body apart.

Than nodded.

Therese's throat tightened. "How?"

"It's better if you don't know."

Tears rushed to Therese's eyes. She was sorry that Hip would have to endure a painful death, and she was even sorrier that her husband would be the one to cause it.

He took her by the hand. "Come on. Let's go."

***

Than led Therese into his father's chambers where he knew his father kept the helm. It was heavily warded to prevent theft, but since Hades trusted his sons, Thanatos was immune to the enchantments.

Guilt flooded him as he set the helm on his head. He'd never taken it before, and—except for the time he broke his oath on the River Styx and made Therese a god—he'd never broken any rules or done anything against his father.

But this time, he felt he had no choice.

He'd heard stories about Circe. She had a way of brainwashing her victims so that even if her spell was broken, her victims wouldn't leave. Than needed to get his brother out of there while Hip still wanted his freedom.

"I can't sense you anymore," Therese said.

Than removed the helm. "You wait here. I'll make this quick."

She arched a brow. "No way. I'm not letting you go alone."

He grabbed her arm and jerked her close. "Do it for the twins, okay?"

Her face softened, and she nodded just before he kissed her.

"Be careful." She threw her arms around his neck. "Please?"

"I will."

Than decided not to mention the fact that he couldn't multiply the helm, because it meant only one of him would be invisible to Circe. Of course, he'd need to disintegrate into two: one to guide his brother's soul and the other to rescue the body.

That was information Therese was better off not knowing. It would only make her worry.

He returned the helm to his head and flew across the sky to Circe's Island.

***

Mrs. Holt emerged from the fitting room with the cream-colored dress Jen had picked out.

Nope. It was one of those that looked better on the rack.

"I don't think so," Jen's mom said with a grin. "What do you think?"

Jen sat back on the bench and shook her head. "Maybe we should try a different store."

"Yeah. I'm too old for this one."

"Mom." Jen rolled her eyes. "You are not *old*."

"Do you realize I turned fifty this year?"

Jen's face fell. With Therese's wedding and Pete's death, they hadn't celebrated her mother's birthday. "I'm sorry we forgot."

"Hell, I even forgot. Pete had just…"

Jen could tell her mother was trying not to cry.

"Am I doing the right thing, baby doll?"

Jen sat up and lifted her chin, trying to read her mother's face. "What do you mean?"

"Getting married again at my age."

Jen's mouth fell open. She couldn't recall her mother ever asking for her advice. With a sinking filling, she realized her mother had always gone to Pete.

"Well, does he make you happy?" Jen looked at her mother sideways.

Mrs. Holt flicked the tears from her cheeks and nodded. "And you gotta know that's hard right now."

"And do you love him?"

Again, Jen's mom nodded. "I really do."

"Then what are you worried about?"

Mrs. Holt glanced around at the few other customers waiting in the fitting room area. "Will you come in the stall and help me with this zipper?"

Jen shrugged. "Sure."

Once they were in the tiny fitting room with the door closed, Mrs. Holt turned to Jen and took both of her hands.

"Listen to me, sweet girl." Jen's mom took a deep breath and let it out before she said, "I need to know if you feel comfortable around John."

"What? Oh…" Jen was so surprised by the question that she didn't know what to say.

"I should have asked you before I said yes, but…"

"Mom. It's okay."

"Seriously, if…"

"Seriously. I mean it. I like Mr. Stern."

Her mother smiled and searched Jen's face. "You do?"

"Yes. What's not to like about him?"

"Well…"

"He helps with the horses, he's nice to you, and he's friendly to me and Bobby, and, well, he's a good guy."

Mrs. Holt released her hands and raked them through her newly dyed hair. "That's all true, baby doll."

"And, to tell you the truth…" Jen hesitated, having second thoughts about what she wanted to say.

"What?"

"I'm actually more comfortable around Mr. Stern than I was around Daddy."

Mrs. Holt's face transformed into despair, and it broke Jen's heart.

"I'm sorry, Mom. I shouldn't have said that."

Her mother wrapped her arms around Jen and broke into tears. "I'll never forgive myself."

Jen fought back tears. "You didn't know."

Her mom held onto Jen for several seconds before she said, "You're right. I didn't know. I should have, but I didn't. And I'm sorry."

"It's okay."

Her mom pulled away to look at her. "No, it's not okay. I'm your mother. I don't know how I was so oblivious." Her face crinkled into a frown. "But what I'm most sorry for is letting him come back…after his therapy."

Jen closed her eyes, trying to fight the tears that wanted to burst like a broken pipe.

"I really thought he was better. I thought the therapy had helped him."

Mrs. Holt wrapped her arms around Jen, and Jen wished she could stay like that in her mother's arms for the rest of the day. How many years had she wished her mother would come to her rescue? Jen had been too afraid, too afraid of getting in trouble to reach out to her mom. When she was little, she thought what had happened between her and her father was her own fault, because back when she was five and six, before she knew it was wrong, she actually…oh, could she admit it? She actually enjoyed it! It was a fun game and she felt special! She thought she was her daddy's favorite. That's what he said, anyway. The tickling and the games and the late-night whisperings were something she looked forward to back then. They'd even sometimes make fun of Bobby or her mom. It was like they were conspiring—partners in crime—and it had been fun.

Jen's tears flowed down her face. She became a mess in her mother's arms as she recalled the days when she first realized what her daddy was doing was bad. And she became so ashamed. She was so ashamed that she didn't dare tell anyone. That's when she started asking him to stop. And he did, for a little while.

But then, his drinking got worse, and, oh! She wanted her mother. She needed her mother. But she was too afraid her mother would hate her if she knew.

"Thank you, Mom," she said now, through her tears. "I'm sorry, too. I'm so sorry I never told you."

"You have nothing to be sorry about, sweet girl. This is all on your dad and me. You are a good girl. A sweet girl. You are my precious girl. You understand?" Her mother lifted Jen's chin.

Jen managed to nod.

"I have always loved you, baby doll, and that will never change."

Jen took a deep breath, and when she let it out, it felt like it went on forever.

They decided not to try another store that day. Instead, they went home. As they drove the winding roads from Durango back toward Lemon Dam, Jen prayed to Hip.

She asked him to please give her a sign that the dream she had had of him was real. Did he really love her? Did he want to be with her for the rest of her life? Or had it just been a dream? A dream from the gates of ivory?

***

Thanatos hadn't been gone long when Hermes appeared and summoned Therese back to Mount Olympus.

"Zeus wants you to accompany the volunteers to interrogate the Hesperides," he explained.

"Why me?"

"He thinks you might be able to use your gifts to make Atlas fall in love with the sheep, like you did with Polyphemus," Hermes explained. "Then maybe Atlas wouldn't be able to use the lightning bolts."

They god traveled to Mount Olympus, where Zeus enlisted her help. Hades was still there, and Therese avoided making eye contact with him, sure she would give away what she and Than had done.

She went with Apollo and Artemis in Apollo's chariot to Morocco, but when they arrived, they found no sheep. The only animal, other than the one-hundred-headed serpent in the tree, was a pig. It was tied to the bottom of the tree, and clearly was not happy about it. Just now as Ares was speaking with the Hesperides, the pig squealed and snorted as though it was aware it was headed for slaughter.

When Therese tried to speak with the pig, she received no answer.

"Where's Atlas?" Artemis asked as the new arrivals approached Ares.

"Atlas?" Ares turned to face them. "What do you want with him?"

The Hesperides scattered, but it was easy for the Olympians to capture them. Therese flew faster than an arrow and grabbed one of the nymphs by her wrist.

Once the daughters of Atlas were tied to the thick roots that lined the ground beneath Ladon's tree, Apollo filled Ares in on what Therese had learned from Polyphemus, and what Thoosa had confessed at court.

Ares swore he was not in cahoots with Atlas.

"You speak the truth," Apollo said. "However, I sense that you did free Atlas with the hope of future conflict."

Ares shrugged. "Guilty as charged. I never thought Atlas had a fighting chance, but I thought it might be interesting to see what he would do."

Artemis put her hands on her hips. "Well, you should be satisfied in knowing that the Titan now has both the trident and a handful of lightning bolts. If he were to ever get the helm…"

"He would be invincible," Apollo finished.

Therese's mouth was suddenly as dry as a stale cracker. She couldn't even swallow. The helm? Could Atlas be after the helm? And was there a remote possibility that her husband was about to enter a trap?

    ***

"Come on, Hypnos. You're no fun," Circe pouted as she ran her fingers through Hip's hair.

Hip laid back on his pillow, closed his eyes, and pretended he was somewhere else. He imagined the bed of leaves near the stream behind Jen's house in the mountains of Colorado. Jen was at his side, stroking his hair. She kissed his shoulder, licked his neck, and whispered in his ear.

"You're so fine."

Okay, maybe that wasn't exactly what Jen would say, but he went with it.

She brushed her lips across his cheek and landed on his mouth. Hip thought only of Jen as he returned the kiss, brought his arms around the warm body that had climbed on top of him.

"I'm sorry to interrupt," came an unfamiliar voice.

Hip opened his eyes and was mortified to see Circe on top of him. A part of him had known it was her, but he'd been thinking of Jen. He was even more mortified to see Atlas standing over them with a mocking look on his face.

"Having fun?" Atlas asked.

"What are you doing here?" Hip demanded.

Circe sat up and used her fingers to tidy her hair. Hypnos wondered why she didn't seem too surprised by Atlas's arrival.

"Were you expecting him?" Hip asked. This could be a good thing. Maybe she would take Atlas as her lover and let Hip go free.

"Your timing is impeccable," Circe said to Atlas, her words laced with sarcasm.

"Go get me one of the sheep," Atlas said. "We need to be ready. He could be coming any day now."

Hip sat up and furrowed his brow. "Who could be coming?"

"Your father," Atlas replied.

Circe left the room, presumably to get a sheep, but why?

"My father?" Hip was completely confused. "What's going on?"

Atlas took a seat at the bedside table and steepled his fingers. "He's coming to recue you because he knows the only way to get past Circe is by using the helm."

"My father's got other things on his mind. I doubt he's coming to rescue me."

"He will eventually," Atlas said. "It may take days, weeks, months…but eventually he'll come for you, and when he does, I'll be waiting."

"That's a foolish plan," Hip said.

"You have no idea," Atlas laughed. "I've had centuries to plan. This one's foolproof."

"So what are you going to do once my father arrives?"

"Steal the helm, of course."

Now it was Hip's turn to laugh. "That's impossible. You won't see him coming, and, as soon as he touches me, we'll both disappear."

Circe returned with a sheep in her arms. "That's where you're wrong."

"How do you figure?" Hip asked as Circe crossed the room and tied the sheep to the bedpost.

Another sheep followed behind, and Atlas shooed it away.

Circe finished the knot and then looked down at Hip. "My spell is too powerful to be broken by even your father. You may become invisible when he touches you, but you won't leave my bed."

"I wouldn't be too sure about that," Hip warned.

"And your father knows this," Atlas added.

Hip shrugged. As Mrs. Holt would say, none of this made a lick of sense. "Then why would he come? Wouldn't it be a waste of his time?"

Atlas leaned forward in his chair. "Your father knows there's only one way to break the spell."

Hip arched a brow.

"He'll have to kill you," Circe said.

"You're forgetting one thing." Hip grinned. "I'm immortal."

"What she means is that your father will have to sever your body from your soul," Atlas explained. "That alone will break Circe's spell."

Hip began to feel faint. "But the only way to do that…"

"Severe damage to the body." Atlas answered for him. "Decapitation is best."

Circe knelt on the bed beside Hip and caressed his cheek. "That's how we'll know you're father's here: when your beautiful head rolls off the bed."

Chapter Eleven: A Trap

Thanatos stood in a copse of trees on the outskirts to the clearing surrounding Circe's house. Luckily the wolves and mountain lions were unaware of his presence. As anxious as he was to save his brother, he was feeling conflicted about this entire mission.

First, he couldn't believe he'd stolen the helm. He'd never done anything like this before, outside of turning Therese. He was always obedient, reliable, and loyal to his parents and to his duties.

Throughout his ancient life, Than had observed that some people were thrilled by breaking the rules, by rebelling against authority, and by being what Hip called a "bad" boy. How many times had Hip teased Than for being too serious?

So here he was being a "bad" boy, breaking a major rule and rebelling against his father's authority, and did he feel excited? Liberated? Thrilled?

Not one bit.

He felt like throwing up.

To make matters worse, in order to save his brother, he'd have to sever Hip's body. The least painful way would be to cut off his head in one clean slice.

Than shuddered as he recalled what Hermes had done for him and Therese not four weeks ago.

So Than felt sick about stealing the helm, and even sicker for what he was about to do to his brother, but he couldn't see any other way to rescue Hip.

And except for Therese, there was no one in the world he loved more.

He took a deep breath, clenched his fists, and headed toward the house.

He was used to not being noticed by most of the life around him as he gathered the souls for the Underworld, but usually an animal or two, and even a human, would turn a head his way, sniff in the air, and know he or she was in the presence of Death. The absolute lack of awareness by any of the mountain lions and wolves in Circe's front yard was jarring. It was the helm, of course. It took some getting used to.

As he stood in the doorway, his eyes were drawn to a magnificent tapestry. It hung in long folds, like thick, heavy curtains, all along the back wall, reaching up to the cathedral ceiling. Centuries of work must have gone into the making of such an enormous fabric.

Everything else in the house was white—even the furniture—except for the black cauldron sitting on the hearth across the room and the witch's grotesque jars lining the shelves.

At the sound of voices, Thanatos turned down the hall to find the bedroom. Hip sat with his back against an iron headboard. Atlas ate at a table next to the bed, and at his feet was a sheep tied to the iron bedpost.

Than suspected it was one of Polyphemus's sheep, and he realized as Circe's laughter rang throughout the room at something clever Hip had no doubt said, that maybe, just maybe, he'd been expected.

He stood there for a long while, taking in the scene.

Hip said, "My father knows better than to walk into this trap you've set for him."

"Make him shut up," Atlas said. "He's trying to warn Hades."

"Unfortunately, I can't put Hypnos to sleep." Circe leaned back on the bed beside Hip and stroked his cheek. "If Thanatos would have been the one to come to me for help, I could have made that brother silent. But this one…well, as long as he's under my spell, no one can sleep, not even Sleep." She cackled at her joke.

"Too bad it wasn't the other brother," Atlas said. "We would have seen faster results. People can afford to go without sleep for a few days, but death cannot wait."

Beneath the helm, Thanatos gnawed on his lower lip. If this was a trap designed for Hades, then that meant Circe had targeted Therese at Scylla's cave, knowing someone from the Underworld would come to the witch to make a deal. Atlas must have enlisted Circe from the beginning. He had lightning bolts, he had the trident, and now he wanted the helm; and here Than was, about to deliver it to him.

Circe pinched Hip's cheek and said, "I'm glad it was this one. I'm rather fond of him."

"Don't get too fond," Atlas said. "We have work to do."

As much as he wanted to save his brother before he was brainwashed into wanting to stay, Than had to go back and report to Mount Olympus, even though he would have to admit that he'd stolen the helm.

It was the right thing to do.

He backed up toward the door and lost his footing. He fell flat on his back as a loose sheep scurried past him. The helm tumbled from his head and slammed against the white marble floor.

Atlas stood from his chair and pointed a thick finger. "Thanatos!"

Circe and Hip both looked at Than in shock.

Circe and Atlas scrambled for the helm.

Thanatos flew and snatched it up just as the other two had nearly reached it. He flew to the ceiling, fumbling with the helm, and finally had it back on. He hid in the corner and waited, panting and full of relief.

"Damn that boy!" Atlas shouted. "He's probably gone to tell the others our plan."

"Quick, give me your sword," Circe said.

"What?" Atlas asked, perplexed.

"Chop off his head, now! Do it!" Circe screamed. "Before Death gets away."

"Now wait a minute," Hip objected, going pale.

"But…"

"He'll have to multiply to recover the body!" Circe explained impatiently. "Give me your sword!"

Circe took the sword from the Titan's sheath, and before Than could do anything to stop her, the witch swung the blade through the air and across Hip's neck.

Than rushed to retrieve his brother's dumbstruck soul, and was about to leave the body for another time, when Circe screeched, "If you leave him here, I'll defile that body in so many horrible ways that you will never be able to reunite it with its soul! I'll boil it and eat it, and then Hip can live inside my gut for the rest of eternity!"

Than disintegrated and flew with haste for the body and the head of his brother, but before he could depart, Atlas paralyzed him with the lightning bolt from the body of the dead sheep lying at his feet.

***

Therese gasped. The duties of death called to her in the way they did whenever Thanatos suffered at the hands of the Maenads. She instantly disintegrated and answered the calls of the dying souls.

And one of them was Hypnos.

Therese found Hypnos, bloody and decapitated, lying next to Than on Circe's bed. She disintegrated, weeping, and, in

146

disbelief, took the soul, body, and head of Hypnos to the Underworld.

Hip, like all souls at death, was confused. She put a comforting hand on his shoulder.

"It's going to be okay," she lied through her tears as she clutched at her lockets.

Another of her carried his broken body to his rooms and gently laid him on his bed. Her tears fell on his lifeless form. She was so sorry. He had gone to help her. At that moment, she vowed she would do whatever she could to make him happy.

Another of her remained behind. She didn't want to put her babies in jeopardy, but the sight of her husband lying motionless on the bed made her freeze, unable to look away.

At the garden of the Hesperides, she turned to Apollo and Artemis with a look that made Ares stop saying whatever it was he had been about to say.

It took her a moment to find the ability to speak.

"Something has happened to Thanatos," she said, as all-out panic overtook her. She forced herself to say this next part, "And he was wearing the helm."

The daughters of Atlas broke out in hideous laughter. The one hundred tongues of Ladon's one hundred heads lashed at them and brought them to silence.

The pig tied at the base of the tree squealed.

In all of the confusion, Therese narrowed her eyes at the pig, wondering why she could not understand what it seemed to be urgently trying to say.

Apollo and his sister rushed to the chariot and called to Therese, but Therese was transfixed by the pig.

It was trying to tell her something.

Therese drew an arrow from her quiver and fitted it to her bow. Then she sent the arrow directly at the pig's heart.

The pig transformed into Amphitrite.

Therese stared back at the goddess, stunned.

Ladon's one-hundred heads attacked Amphitrite at the same time Ares whipped out his sword and lashed at the serpent's necks. Therese fitted another arrow and turned the giant beast into a tiny canary, his fallen heads becoming feathers floating through the air.

"The trident!" Amphitrite cried. "It's hidden in the tree!"

Ladon returned to his normal form before anyone could react. Therese fitted another arrow and turned him into a fish. He landed at the base of the tree, causing the Hesperides to shriek.

Apollo, by this time, had reached the tree and found the trident, but it disappeared before he laid hands on it.

"Atlas is here with the helm!" Therese shouted, because that was the only explanation for the trident's sudden disappearance. "He has the trident!"

Poseidon appeared, roaring like a train.

Therese moved just in time to avoid getting zapped from the invisible source of the trident. To protect her babies, she god travelled away and hoped and prayed the others got out safely, too.

Back at Circe's house, Therese watched as the witch stirred the brew in her cauldron in the main part of her house.

"I know you're here," Circe said. "Go ahead and take him. He's no good to me in that condition, anyway." The witch cackled.

Therese hesitated, fearing a trap, but her need to hold Than in her arms won out, and she flew to him.

***

Hypnos had never been more relieved to find himself in Tartarus. He just hoped his body was somewhere safe. He prayed to his brother and got no reply. He prayed to Therese, who appeared to him instantly.

As he listened to her explain through her tears what had happened, first at Circe's after his death and then at the Garden of the Hesperides, Hypnos could not keep his transparent mouth from hanging open.

"I'm watching over Thanatos, now, not sure what to do. I'm also on my way to Mount Olympus," Therese explained. "I'll fill you in when I know more."

Therese vanished.

She hadn't been gone a full minute when Hip heard a loud roar, like a train, from somewhere in Tartarus. He flew to the main hall, where his sisters tormented their victims. Meg looked up at him as he entered, wearing the same look of confusion on her face that he was likely wearing on his.

"What was that?" he asked.

"I don't know."

They waited, listening.

"Help!" cried the scratchy voice of Melinoe the Malevolent. "I can't hold them back any longer!"

Hypnos prayed to his father as he and Meg rushed to the deepest pit.

Soon Tizzie was at his heels. "What's going on?"

"We don't know," was all he could say as they clambered down the winding pit as fast as they could—it was dangerous to god travel this deep without knowing what dangers lay ahead.

As they neared the bottom, where the great iron door imprisoned the Titans, they were shocked to see Melinoe and a handful of souls flying in circles around the door.

"Someone's in here!" Melinoe cried. "We can't sense him, but he's been shooting something powerful at this door!"

Hades appeared. "It's Atlas, no doubt."

"You're right about that!" came the voice of the Titan.

As soon as the Titan had spoken, the other gods detected his location and converged upon him in a heap. Hades managed to recover his helm, but not before Atlas shot the iron door with both the trident and a lightning bolt in a powerful explosion that sent everything and everyone flying.

Because Hypnos had no corporeal body, he and the other souls who had gathered there were not affected by the blast. They watched in silent terror as Atlas returned to the bottom of the pit, reached in his stout arm, and pulled his brother Menoetius out.

The shouts from the other Titan prisoners rang out in the pit, but before the Titans could make their escape, an invisible force shoved the iron door closed.

Hypnos knew it was his father, wearing his helm.

But Atlas took the trident and pointed it at the iron door. "It's no use, Hades!" the Titan cried. "You can close it as often as you like, but I'm only going to keep busting it back open."

Hip wished there was something he could do to help—anything.

As Atlas directed the force of the trident toward the iron door, Melinoe appeared in front of him and took the full paralyzing force with her own body.

This gave Meg, Tizzie, and Hades time to act. Hypnos watched in helpless wonder as the arm holding the trident was cut from its body, the trident was recovered by the invisible Hades, and Atlas was bound with the thick chains of the Furies.

Atlas had been captured, but his brother, Menoetius, was no longer in sight, and Melinoe lay in a heap on the ground.

***

Jen led Ace at a walk back to the pen. Bobby was right behind her on Hershey. Their mother and John—that's what they were asked to call Mr. Stern—had already gone indoors to prepare supper. Apparently they wanted to talk about the ceremony and wanted all of them together.

Times like tonight made Jen miss Pete.

Bobby must have been thinking along the same lines, because when he came into the barn where she was removing tack and putting it away, he asked, "Can you talk to Pete?"

"Nuh-uh. I wish." She took a brush to Ace's back.

Bobby got to work on Hershey. "Could you get a message to him?"

She looked up, her brows bent. "I suppose. Why?"

"I want him to know I'm sorry."

"For what?"

"For blaming him. When Daddy had to leave. I told Pete it was his fault."

"Oh."

Tears built up in his eyes, visible beneath his cowboy hat even in the fading light. "I owe both of you an apology. I just…"

"It's okay," Jen said, not really wanting to talk about it. "I understand."

"You do?"

She nodded. "So will Pete. I'll make sure of it."

Bobby smiled, but not at her. He was embarrassed and awkward, but Jen knew how much courage he'd needed to bring it up to her. She was sorry to realize how heavily it had still weighed on his mind, and, at that moment, she realized she had never been her father's only victim. They'd all suffered. This made her feel sad, but it also brought her some comfort. She wasn't alone. She had her mother and brothers.

Bobby finished up and headed to the house to wash up. She took her time in the barn, even though she didn't like being alone in there anymore—not since her father's ghost had haunted it. She could never sense him, but she suspected he was there. She was tired of being afraid of him.

"You were selfish," she said out loud, in case he was there and could hear her. "You should have tried to get help sooner—if it was a sickness. You should have done it for us. For me."

She turned out the light and quickly left the barn. Her heart was beating fast, but she shed no tears. She refused to cry, ever again, about him and what he'd done. The past was the past. Now she'd said her peace. It was over.

As she crossed the gravel path toward her house, a huge wind picked up and threw dirt against her body, stinging her eyes. She shut them, bringing her hands to her face. Then something powerful lifted her up off of the ground and dragged her through the air. She screamed.

If this was Hip's way of sweeping her off her feet, she was going to kill him.

Chapter Twelve: Menoetius

As soon Therese reached Thanatos in Circe's bed, an invisible force pushed her onto the covers beside him.

"What do you want?" Therese shouted at Circe, unable to free herself from the bed.

Circe laughed her evil laugh—more like a cackle.

Therese's power of disintegration came to an abrupt halt. She had just reached the gates of Mount Olympus, had just left the Garden of the Hesperides, had just ushered two hundred and fifty-eight thousand souls to the Underworld, only to find herself sucked from all those locations back to this one spot on the witch's bed.

Before she had time to wonder who would take over the duties of Death, a powerful gust of wind blew the bottom of the covers up and over her head. Minutes went by before she could push the covers back down, despite her efforts. When she finally did succeed in shoving the blanket from her head, she found herself lying beside Than on the hard floor of a grotto behind a thick waterfall. The roar of the falls made it difficult to hear anything else.

The bed was gone, but the top cover remained, her legs entangled in the blue cotton blanket embroidered with tiny birds.

"Than?" She put her ear to his chest and held her breath.

His heartbeat was faint, but at least he had one. She could also feel the shallow rise and fall of his breathing.

"Than, can you hear me?" She could hardly hear herself.

When he gave no answer, she looked around to assess her surroundings, praying to every god and goddess she knew. She had a feeling none could hear her, because she heard no one answering. She walked to the lip of the grotto and looked over the edge where the water pooled into a rushing stream several yards below. To her left was a smaller waterfall, and, down below, an even deeper canyon floor.

She knew that canyon. She knew these falls. She'd been here before.

She stood there with her mouth open for several long seconds, totally confused.

She stopped breathing.

She and Than were in the battlefield where she fought against McAdams four years ago.

***

Hunched over Melinoe, Hypnos watched as the Furies carried Atlas up from the pit to the main hall of Tartarus and bound the Titan to one of their tables of torture. Melinoe's soul had not been severed from her body, but she, nevertheless, seemed lifeless. She'd been paralyzed by the trident.

Hades removed his helm and joined him near the Malevolent.

"How long will she be like this?" Hip asked his father.

Hades bowed his head. "One never knows. In some cases, a direct hit from the trident has caused permanent damage."

"Poor Melinoe." Hip reached out and touched her hair, but of course, his transparent hand fell through her.

Hades lifted her up and carried her to a table in the main hall, next to the angry Titan.

"It's too late, Hades," Atlas said. "My plan is already in motion. I don't need the trident or your silly helm."

"It wasn't so silly when you went to great measures to steal it," Hades said, as he arranged Melinoe's arms at her side and turned his attention to Atlas.

Hip stood over Melinoe, still in awe of what she had done. He wondered why she had done it, when she had nothing to gain. Was it possible that his sister had feelings for her family after all?

Tizzie and Meg were in their full state as avengers—hair turned to snakes, blood seeping from their eyes and mouths. Meg knelt on the Titan's chest with her falcon perched on her shoulder, ready to peck out his eyes at a moment's notice. Tizzie stood alongside him with her wolf on her left, baring his sharp teeth. She had her whip wrapped tightly around her right hand. She lashed the end of it against the Titan's legs. When he laughed, she did it more fiercely, repeatedly, until blood and skin hung from his shins and his laughter turned to pleading.

"Where is your brother, Menoetius?" Hades insisted.

"How should I know?"

Meg's falcon swooped in and took out the Titan's left eye. He groaned.

"How's your memory now?" Meg hissed, her blood dripping onto his face and mixing with his.

"Stop!" Atlas pleaded. "I don't know! I swear on the River Styx, I don't know where my brother is."

"You better tell us what you do know!" Meg growled. "Or you'll lose your other eye!"

"Of course, it *will* grow back," Hades said rather calmly.

Meg smiled at her father. "That's right. So my falcon can do it again!"

When Atlas said nothing, Tizzie struck him again with her whip.

Hypnos had never watched his sisters at work for any length of time. Now he remembered why.

"It won't do you any good to know," Atlas growled. "The plan is already underway."

"Then you may as well tell us," Hades said in that eerily calm voice that Hip recalled from when he was a child and his father scolded him.

The falcon dipped its beak, ready to strike.

"Okay! Okay!" Atlas cried, panting. "This is what I know!"

Hypnos moved closer to his father and the Titan.

"We're listening," Tizzie said.

Her wolf howled.

"When Ares freed me, I went to Circe. I didn't know where else to go."

"And?" Hades prompted.

"And apparently she has a thing for Menoetius. She cooked up a plan to help him escape."

"Are you saying this was Circe's plan from the beginning?" Hades asked.

Atlas nodded. "She told me to take the credit. I was happy to."

Hypnos couldn't believe he'd been in the arms of the mastermind behind the plot against his family. "Swear on the River Styx," he insisted.

"I swear," the Titan said.

"So your brother is likely with the witch now," Meg speculated.

"Maybe," Atlas said. "But maybe not."

"Where else might he be?" Hades demanded.

Sweat had broken out on the Titan's skin. "He's setting traps."

Meg and Tizzie exchanged worried glances. Even though he had no body, Hypnos had the sensation of a shudder crawling down his back.

"For whom?" Hades asked.

"For all of you," Atlas said. "He and Circe are going to trap you all."

***

The violent wind lifted Jen over the treetops and spun her around and around. She was dizzy, panting, unable to see. She cried out for Hip, then for Therese, then for her mom. After several terrifying minutes of screaming at the top of her lungs, she landed at the base of a tree on a bed of dried leaves. A bruised apple lay at her feet.

An enormous shadow was cast on the ground beside the apple. Trembling with fear, she slowly looked up to see a giant standing over her. She froze, utterly helpless, utterly defenseless.

He looked like a human, except gigantic and stout. Black hair fell into his eyes, which glared down at her with anger.

What had Therese gotten her mixed up in now?

"When they ask you who brought you here, you tell them it was Menoetius."

She wanted to ask where in the world she was, but she didn't dare. She looked up at him and nodded, her mouth hanging open like a panting dog.

The giant turned his back on her and disappeared.

Jen scrambled to her feet and backed up against the tree, looking in all directions. Who would ask her who had brought her here? Was there someone else in these woods?

As she combed the area for clues of her whereabouts, she caught sight of about a dozen sharp sticks jutting out of the ground a few yards from where she was standing. They were covered in what appeared to be dried blood and more dead leaves.

What was this place?

Terrified of walking in the woods, where there might be more sharpened sticks less visible, Jen hugged the tree. She looked up. Apples hung from the branches—some green, but others perfectly ripe. Across from it was an orange tree. Whose fruit orchard was this? No one living around Lemon Dam had a fruit orchard. Did that mean the wind had carried her far away from home?

She heard the snap of twigs and froze. She held her breath and listened. When she heard the sound again, she reached up to the lowest branches of the tree and climbed as high as she could. Sucking in air, she glanced all around, searching for the thing she knew was in the woods.

***

Thanatos couldn't move. He couldn't even open his eyes. He lay on his back on a hard surface—he knew that much—and he could hear the thundering sound of falling water. The air was humid but not hot. He sensed filtered light touching his eyelids. A thin blanket lay over his body, and beside him, something moved.

"Than, can you hear me?"

It was Therese. If he could have sighed with relief, he would have. Her soft, warm hand touched his cheek. He could feel her breath on his face. He wanted to kiss her.

"Oh, honey, I wish you'd wake up," she said.

He *was* awake. He tried to move his mouth to say it. He focused, strained…nothing.

"How did we end up here?" she said. "Of all places?"

A surge of adrenaline pumped through him. Where were they? And why was Therese so concerned?

Her face move closer to his, as though she were studying him. Her breath smelled of cinnamon and cherries. Her mouth was close.

She whispered, "Oh, Than."

Her lips caressed his cheek. He felt something move deep inside him. Then she brought her mouth to his, planting soft and sweet kisses. Unexpectedly, she nipped his lower lip, and something woke up deep in his belly. Her tongue traced the line where his lips met. He thought he would explode.

At last, he could open his eyes.

Therese didn't notice right away. He still couldn't speak or move. He watched the top of her head as she traced her mouth along his chin and down his neck, to the spot just below his Adam's apple. He swallowed hard.

That's when she looked up at him and saw his opened eyes.

"Than! Oh, sweetheart! You're awake!"

He blinked. The corners of his mouth twitched, but that was as much movement as he was able to make.

She ran her hands through his hair and kissed his forehead, his cheeks, and his mouth. "Thank the gods!" she said over and over. "Thank the gods!"

He enjoyed every minute of it.

"Oh, I was so worried."

The last he recalled was being struck by Atlas with a lightning bolt. The memories flooded him. What had happened to Hip? Did Atlas have the helm? He had so many questions. Surely, Therese would know of his questions.

"You won't believe where we are," she said.

He sensed reluctance in her voice.

He closed his eyes, trying to be patient.

"We're in my battlefield, where I fought McAdams."

Than's eyes flew open. What were they doing there?

"I don't have a clue how it's possible, but I recognize this place. Believe me. I couldn't forget it if I tried."

Circe sent them here. That made sense. This battlefield had been a gift from her to the Olympians—a peace offering after her role in the clash with the Titans. She must have reclaimed it from Zeus and has now made it their prison. But why, and for how long?

"I took Hip's body—all of it—to his bed. And I took his soul to Tartarus," she finally said. "As soon as I came for you, we were transported here."

Than was relieved that his brother was safe at home and out of the clutches of the witch. At least not all of Therese's news was bad.

"The last thing I saw before the witch trapped me," Therese continued, "was Atlas wearing the helm and snatching the trident from Hera's apple tree."

Than closed his eyes and filled with guilt. If only he hadn't stolen the helm. Now everything and everyone was at risk because of his foolishness.

Chapter Thirteen: The Wait

Jen held her breath and listened for the thing moving below her in the woods. Straining her eyes, she peered through the branches. Whatever it was, it wasn't human.

The beast took another step—just a few more and it would be directly below her. Jen tried not to move, but her hands were shaking the branches.

As the beast moved to the base of the tree, Jen couldn't believe her eyes. The corners of her mouth lifted into a smile of relief. The beast below her was a horse, and it was eating the apples on the ground.

As quietly as she could, Jen crept down the tree and stepped onto the leaves below. The horse noticed her right away, but it continued to chomp and stare at her.

"Hello there," Jen said, in her gentlest voice, to what she was fairly certain was a mare. "Aren't you a pretty thing?"

Its chocolate coat glistened in the light filtering through the trees.

Jen moved closer, careful to stay in the animal's limited line of vision. She didn't want to spook it.

"I wonder where you came from," Jen said sweetly.

She plucked a ripe apple from one of the lower branches and offered it to the mare. The horse sniffed her hand and then took the apple. Jen stroked the side of the horse's face and sighed.

"Are we friends now?" Jen asked.

The horse found another apple on the ground near Jen's feet and ate it. Jen stood still, giving the animal time to become more accustomed to her. There was no place else she'd rather be in these mysterious woods than on a horse's back—if only the mare would cooperate.

Jen had never ridden without tack, so she studied the mare for a few minutes, wondering how best to mount her. Luckily, the animal wasn't huge. She was about the same size as Sugar. Jen stroked the animal's neck and then gradually made her way to its back. She seemed to be used to people. Jen wondered if she was on someone else's property petting someone else's horse.

"I don't think you're a wild thing," Jen murmured.

She reached her arms along the horse's back and stood there embracing the mare, making sure the horse was comfortable.

"Who do you belong to then?" Jen asked.

Jen spotted a big rock a few yards away. Maybe if she stood on the rock, it would give her enough lift to swing a leg around. Now the only question was, could she lift that rock?

Slowly, she stepped around the tree toward the rock. The bottom of her boot hooked on something jutting out of the ground, and Jen fell on her hands and knees.

It hurt like hell, but she didn't want to scare away the horse, so she bit down on her bottom lip instead. She'd fallen in a shallow hole of pointy sticks. Most of them were broken and covered in dried blood, but two of them scraped her and tore her flesh—one on her knee and the other on her hand. Who on earth would set such treacherous traps, especially with animals around?

She climbed to her feet and limped over to the big rock. She dug around it to loosen it from the earth and then cupped her hands beneath it. It was heavy, like the old television they had before they got their flat screen, but Jen could lift it. Careful to avoid the trap, she returned to the base of her tree, where the horse was still eating.

She set the rock on the ground beside the horse, talking sweetly the whole while, even though she still wanted to grunt and growl over the stinging pain in her knee and hand.

"You're okay, sweet thing," she said.

Then she leaned her trunk against the horse's mane and swung her leg over its back. The horse moved forward and back, as though unused to riders, but it didn't buck or run.

"Steady, girl," Jen said. "I'm not gonna hurt ya."

She wrapped her arms around the horse's neck, feeling safer already.

"That's a good girl," Jen cooed.

Even though light continued to flicker down from the sky, Jen was so sleepy. She closed her eyes, took a deep breath in and out, and relaxed against the mare.

***

When the Furies had squeezed as much information as they could from their prisoner, Hades summoned Hermes to invite the other gods to conduct their own interrogations. Hermes returned to request that the prisoner be brought to Mount Olympus.

"The others aren't comfortable here," the messenger god explained.

Hypnos rolled his transparent eyes. After all the work the Alliance did together in the Underworld, they were still snobby about meeting here?

"But it's risky to transport Atlas with Menoetius and Circe at large," Hades objected. "The witch's black magic is powerful."

"And they still have the lightning bolts," Hip added.

"I'll give them your reply," Hermes said. "Poseidon may already be on his way. He's anxious to get his trident."

"Let me in!" Poseidon's voice came from above.

Hip had forgotten that only Hermes had the trust of his father. Powerful wards kept the other Olympians from travelling in and out at will.

Hades lifted his hand, and Poseidon appeared before them just as Hermes took his leave.

"Where is it?" the god of the sea asked.

Hades pointed to the table across the room. "It's protected by ancient runes." Hades crossed the room and used his sword to scratch out the marks on the table.

"I'm beholden to you, brother," Poseidon said as he took the trident in his hands.

Hades gave him a nod. Hip had never seen affection exchanged between his father and uncle. He supposed this was as good as it ever got for them.

"We must all work together to defeat our common enemies," Hades said. "Do you want to question the prisoner?"

"I want to do more than question him!" Poseidon replied. "Let me at him!"

After Poseidon had culled the same information from the Titan as the Furies had, other gods began to arrive, and, one by one, Hades let them in. Apollo came first, followed by his sister. Then came Athena and her mother. Hera and Rhea were next. The last to arrive was Hephaestus.

Hip didn't expect Aphrodite or Hestia to come, but he was disappointed that his mother was not among them. When he prayed to Hermes about it, the messenger god said that Demeter refused to come, and she refused to let her daughter leave her side.

"What about Zeus?" Hades asked out loud. "Is he not coming?"

Hermes shook his head.

"He can't stand it here," Hera explained. "He sends his apologies. I'm here in his place."

"And Ares?" Hades asked.

The other gods glanced silently at one another.

Then Athena said, "He's under house arrest at the moment because of his role in freeing Atlas."

The Titan, who'd been quiet on his table of torture, laughed.

Hip decided to leave the main hall. It was too crowded and complicated for his tastes. He'd heard enough, anyway. He decided to go to the seers' pit. He wanted to question Pete about what he'd seen the day Jen and her family had visited.

On the way, he came across Hecate escorting a soul.

"Are you acting as Death?" Hip asked.

"Yes," she said. "What's happened to Thanatos and Therese?"

"Than was hit by one of Atlas's lightning bolts," he said. "Therese went to get him. Something must have gone wrong."

If Hip had had a heart, it would have felt heavy. He was anxious to find out what had happened to his two best friends.

"If I learn anything, I'll let you know," Hecate said as she moved on with the mortal soul.

Pete was speaking with Tiresias when Hip entered the pit where the Phlegethon did not flow. Pete appeared to be recovered from his strange episode during the Holts' visit.

Pete sensed him immediately and left the other seer's side.

"Hello, Hypnos," Pete said.

"You feeling okay?" Hip asked.

"Better."

They sat down on rocks.

"You want to know what I saw," Pete said.

"Unless you don't think you can…"

"It's okay. I was just telling Tiresias about it. I can't make sense of it. It was a shock. I'm not sure what it means."

"What was it?" Hip asked. "What was the vision?"

"Well, Jen gave me her blood wanting me to tell her about her future."

"So?" Hip shifted nervously on the rock.

"Well, I didn't see her future. I saw mine."

"Oh. What did you see?" A tinge of disappointment mixed with relief snaked down the place where Hip's spine would have been.

"I was standing before my father's ghost. He was bowing before me, like I was a god, like I was the god of death. I put my hand on his shoulder and led him here, where he was sentenced to Tartarus. I watched as Tizzie and her sisters tormented him. But I watched with my eyes. They had returned to my sockets."

"Where was my brother?" Hip asked, concerned.

"I don't know," Pete said. "He wasn't in the vision."

"Why did that freak you out?" Hip asked. "If you are one day able to bring your father here…"

"But that's all impossible, don't you see? It makes me think I've lost the sight. I'm confusing fantasy now with truth."

"You don't know that."

"How could I ever be, even for a moment, the lord of death?"

Another shiver worked its way down Hip's transparent back. Therese had gone to get his brother hours ago. Any prayers he tried to send their way remained unanswered.

What if Than never recovered from the lightning bolt?

***

Thanatos wished he could lift his arms and wrap them around Therese. She lay beside him, her cheek on his chest. He could smell her clean hair. She'd been quiet for a while, but now she lifted her face to his and asked, "Are you thirsty?"

He actually was. His throat was as dry as the bottom of a cracker barrel. He blinked once.

She climbed to her feet and returned in a moment with her hands cupped together, cold water dripping onto him. Her arms were soaked, and droplets of water clung to her lashes and nose.

As she leaned over him, the cold water trickled down his neck. Very little made it through his lips and down his throat, but it was enough.

He looked up at her with gratitude, willing her to lean closer and put her lips to his. They hadn't been able to communicate through prayer. He supposed it was because he was paralyzed.

"Do you want some more?"

He didn't blink. This was his way of saying no.

She understood. "Are you hungry?"

Again, he didn't blink. He was able to go a long time without food.

"I think I should look around. What do you think?"

No. He couldn't say it, but he kept his eyes from blinking. He wished he could tell her how much he thought that was a bad idea. Why go looking for trouble? If trouble was out there, they might as well wait for it to come to them.

"I don't know if you've noticed, but my belly is a lot bigger." She stood over him. "See the hump?"

He blinked. Yes, he did see the hump. She looked adorable. He wished he could reach up his hands to her hump and maybe feel one or both of the twins touch him back.

"Whoa!" she cried with a laugh. "They're really busy in there. They must be wrestling!"

He wished he could laugh. It didn't matter that he couldn't move. This was one of the happiest moments of his life. His beautiful wife standing over him talking about their rambunctious babies inside of her couldn't be more wonderful.

173

Well, he supposed being able to embrace them would be nice. And knowing that they were safe would be nicer still. But he'd take what he could get.

He watched as she stood at the edge of the grotto, looking out. He wondered what she could see. He didn't blame her for wanting to explore. He knew he would if he were the one who could walk. But he hoped she wouldn't, for the sake of the babies.

"I'm hungry." She turned to face him, speaking loudly over the falls. "I don't know if it's because of the babies, or what, but I'm really hungry."

He gazed at her back as she continued. "And I didn't want to tell you this, but..." She paused.

For heaven's sake, he wanted to say. How could she do that to him? Spit it out!

"But, well, I don't know why, but I seem to have lost my ability to fly."

She turned to him and knelt at his side, her face twisted with worry.

"And I feel weak," she continued. "Like I've lost all of my power. Do you think it's the pregnancy?"

He didn't know. Dear gods, he didn't know. He'd never felt more helpless. One minute, he was basking in the beauty of his pregnant wife, and now he was watching her go crazy with worry. Talk about mood swings.

She got up and went back to the edge of the grotto. "I wonder how long we'll be trapped here. How long before someone rescues us?"

He squeezed his eyes shut. Even if he could speak, he had no answer. It was highly possible that no one except Circe knew where they were.

***

Therese stared down at the canyon floor. She could vividly recall McAdams scrambling down for what she thought was her shield only to see him clutch the apple core she had discarded from her decoy camp after having eaten several pieces of fruit. Trembling and ravenous, like a wild, starved animal, McAdams had eaten the whole thing, stem and all.

And now she stood at the lip of the grotto four years later as though nothing had changed. No, that wasn't true. A lot had changed. She was more confident, more purposeful, and more sure about what was important to her than she'd ever been. Four years ago, she'd been a desperate, frightened, and grieving fifteen-year-old, and now she was a protector of animals, a wife, and mother-to-be, unafraid to fight for what she believed in.

She gazed across the canyon to the platform on the other side, where the gods had watched her battle with McAdams. She shivered as she recalled how upset Hades had been when she had failed to strike the mortal blow. But even today, she would refuse to kill a helpless person, no matter what heinous acts that person had committed. The difference between today and four years ago was that today she would stand up more firmly for what she believed.

As much as she had grown to love Hades, his refusal to consider changing the ancient laws for Melinoe and Pete—and even poor, old Tiresias—made her that much more determined to fight him. In her gut, she knew all souls deserved the chance to move on.

After all, the Athena Alliance had been successful in reforming Mount Olympus. If she and the others could convince Zeus to change his ways, then she felt confident she could do the same with Hades.

Hopefully, that wouldn't require a war.

These thoughts of bravado would come to nothing, however, if she and Than were never rescued. Losing the abilities of prayer and flight on top of losing her strength made her suspect that something more than her pregnancy was the cause. Maybe Circe had enchanted this battlefield in a way that drained those in it of their powers. And what if Than never fully recovered from the direct hit of the lightning bolt?

Four years ago, in the aftermath of her parents' murder, she might have given up. But today, she knew that more than flight, more than strength, more than all the abilities of a god, hope was the most important thing in the world. She covered her growing belly with her hands and promised her babies that she would never give up hope.

Something moving to her left caught her attention and brought her from her reverie. She squinted and shielded her eyes from the sun, which remained at high noon despite the passing of time. The moving figure was a horse, but there was someone on its back. Therese held her breath as the horse walked along Aphrodite's stream in the upper canyon.

The horse bent over the stream to take a drink. When it did, the person looked up and saw Therese standing at the edge of the grotto. Therese froze. She couldn't believe she had allowed herself to be seen. Adrenaline surged through her until the person waved an arm and shouted across the canyon.

"Therese!"

Therese's mouth fell open. She knew that voice.

"Jen?"

The person waved both arms and shouted again, "Therese! It's me, Jen!"

To Than, Therese said, "How did *she* get here?"

Chapter Fourteen: Death Trap

Therese reached a hand down to Jen and helped her up and over the edge of the grotto. The brown horse continued down the canyon toward Poseidon's river.

"How did you get here?" Therese asked.

"A giant named Minnoshus, or something. I've been scared out of my mind. Can you take me home?"

Therese glanced over to where Than lay paralyzed a few feet away.

Jen followed Therese's gaze. "Oh, no. Is he okay?"

Therese sucked in her lips and tried not to cry. Now that her friend was here to feel sorry for her, the waterworks threatened to pour.

Jen knelt at Than's side and leaned over him. "You're awake."

"He was paralyzed by a lightning bolt," Therese explained, as she knelt on the other side of Than from Jen. "He can't speak."

"But this isn't the first time." Jen put a hand to Than's forehead, as though checking for fever. "He was struck last year and recovered."

"True. I'm hoping he does again."

"But you seem worried."

"This was a more direct hit," Therese said. Then, not wanting to upset him, she added, "But I'm sure he'll be fine." She leaned over and kissed her husband's cheek.

"So why are we here?" Jen asked.

"That's the million dollar question."

Just then, they both heard a faint shout from the canyon below. They looked at each other for a moment.

"Who's that?" Jen whispered.

Therese shook her head as the shout came again, barely audible through the roar of the falls.

"Sounds like a woman," Jen whispered.

"Wait here." Therese got up and peered from behind the falls over the grotto's edge.

The voice came again—not from below, but across the canyon where the gods had assembled four years ago. A figure—a woman with white and black hair—was scaling the wall and had reached the summit.

It was Hecate. She bent over, panting, hands on her knees. Apparently she was without her goddess strength, too.

Therese shouted her name.

Twenty minutes later, after climbing back down from the platform, across the canyon, and up the ledge behind the falls, Hecate joined Therese and Jen on the hard ground at Than's side.

"How did you get here?" Therese asked the goddess.

"I went to collect a soul and found Menoetius and Circe waiting for me."

"But why?" Therese asked.

"I heard they mean to trap us all," Hecate said.

"Us who?" Jen asked.

"The Olympians," Hecate replied.

"Then why Jen?" Therese asked.

"Leverage, perhaps," Hecate guessed.

***

Hypnos was relieved when, a week after his brutal murder, his body finally called to his soul, and they were one again. But no sooner had this happened then the duties of Death beckoned.

To Hecate, he sent a prayer of sarcasm: *Sorry to relieve you of your favorite post,* but he got nothing in reply. Maybe she didn't appreciate his sense of humor.

Hecate?

Still no reply.

Mother, have you seen Hecate?

Not since she took over for Thanatos a week ago. Why? And have you heard from him yet?

No.

We've combed the ends of the earth looking for him and Therese, his mother said. *We're running out of ideas. Please help us as soon as you can.*

As Hip had this telepathic conversation with his mother, he disintegrated and answered the call from souls all over the world. One in particular worried him, because it was calling from the Holts' place.

Fortunately, he could sense it wasn't Jen, but the idea of her family going through another tragedy made him want to wring the necks of all three Fates. As he arrived, he could tell with some relief that the soul was animal, not human.

It was the goat that was sometimes tied to the front of the house. Its head had been cut clean off and the body left to rot. Who would do such a thing?

As soon as he reached it, a puff of bitter powder accosted him from all directions, and, as he blinked and wiped his eyes, someone grabbed him.

He opened his eyes to find Circe standing before him with that wry grin.

"Hello, Hypnos," she said.

He struggled against whoever had pinned his arms behind his back.

"That's Menoetius," Circe said. "We thought you'd like to know that we've got your little girlfriend."

Hip flailed his body against the implacable force that was the Titan. Circe's black magic must have been at work; otherwise, the struggle would be less one-sided. "Why are you doing this?"

"I saw your dream, young god," Circe taunted. "As I curled my fingers in your pretty golden hair and put my lips against your tasty mouth, you were dreaming of that mortal girl instead of relishing what was right there with you!"

Hip narrowed his eyes. "Jealous much?" The witch was insane.

Circle cackled. "Don't flatter yourself." Then she added, "But if you want *her* so badly, you can have her."

"Why are you doing this? What do you want?" As Hip spoke, he found he could not communicate through prayer.

"I want every one of your kind imprisoned," she replied.

The world opened up, and water rushed at him, sucking him down in a whirlwind of confusion. He floundered, unable to breathe and unable to keep his head afloat. He hated water! And now it seemed it would be the death of him. He wasn't ready to return to Tartarus. He fought, struggled, kicked, pulled, and held his breath, but found his strength zapped away.

He stopped kicking and opened his eyes, reminding himself to focus and remain calm. He assessed his surroundings and was at last able to see which way was up and which was down. Flattening his arms to his sides, he allowed himself to sink to the bottom. Then, once his boots struck ground, he pushed as hard as he could and flung himself to the surface.

For the brief seconds his head emerged, he spotted land. He snatched a gulp of air and then kicked and paddled as best as he could toward the shore. This seemed to take forever, and when he finally felt the smooth hot surface of rock, he pulled himself from the miserable water and kissed the land.

As soon as he noticed the raised platform overlooking the river from which he had just emerged, he squinted in bewilderment. What on earth was he doing in Zeus's battlefield?

***

Because the sun always shone, even filtered, as it was, by the falls at the opening of the grotto, Thanatos could not tell how many days and nights he had been lying paralyzed with Therese, Jen, and Hecate looking after him. It had been long enough that he knew he was hungry. It had been long enough that Therese's abdomen had grown to twice the size it had been when he had first opened his eyes. It had been long enough.

He had made *some* progress. He was able to wiggle his toes and fingers, and, although he still could not move his lips, he could clear his throat and make sounds to get the women's attention. They brought him water when he needed it, which hadn't been often. Therese had even squeezed a bit of orange juice into his mouth from the stash Jen and Hecate had gathered during one of their excursions into Demeter's woods. He tried to consume as little as possible, not knowing what he would do if he needed to empty his bladder.

He had to admit he rather liked the feeling of Therese lying beside him the two times she had rested. In addition to the even rise and fall of her breath and the silky smooth warmth of her face nestled against his neck, he'd been able to feel the babies moving and kicking about. While this brought him immeasurable joy, he was afraid they might want to be born while they were still trapped in this insane prison. Although Therese had rested twice, Jen had slept—albeit restlessly—a half a dozen times, which led him to suspect a week or more had passed.

One good thing that had come from this situation was the opportunity for Therese to spend time with Jen. He was reminded of how much the two girls cared about one another. Just now, Jen was telling the other two women about her ideas for a baby shower. Jen seemed to forget altogether that they were trapped in a prison and not at a week-long sleepover.

"I haven't even told Carol and Richard yet," Therese admitted.

This made Than frown, which, in turn made him smile. He was able to move his mouth! Could he speak?

"Why not?" Jen asked.

Than watched Therese carefully as she glanced his way before saying, "I just haven't had time."

"Tell me the truth, girlfriend," Jen said. "I can tell you're lying. Hecate, do you know?"

Hecate shrugged. "I can think of a number of reasons."

"She's frightened," Than said.

Therese sprang to her feet and hovered over him. "You can speak!" She knelt and hugged his waist. "How do you feel?"

"Frustrated. What about you? Are you okay?"

She nodded before covering his mouth with hers. He relished in the ability to finally kiss her back.

Hecate and Jen had knelt beside him, too, and he looked up at them self-consciously before ending his kiss.

"What about the babies?" he asked.

"They're huge." She sat up and showed off her beach-ball-sized belly.

"I noticed. I can't believe it."

"Do you want anything?" Therese asked. "Food, orange juice, water?"

"No. I'm okay." Then he added, "Hello, Jen. Hello, Hecate."

"Hello," they both replied.

"Do you have any idea why Circe and Menoetius are doing this to us?" Therese asked.

His theory was that Circe planned to overthrow the Olympians, but he didn't want to upset Therese, so he said, "I'm not sure."

The women made themselves comfortable on the ground around him, apparently planning on including him now in their talk.

"Not to change the subject," Jen started, "but why would Therese be scared to tell her aunt and uncle about the babies? They'll be thrilled."

Than explained about the prophecy, about the babies being mortal, and about the problem of what to do.

"Hera and Hestia said I should give them up," Therese said. "That mortals should be raised by mortals."

"Maybe your aunt and uncle could adopt them," Jen suggested. "At least they'd still be in the family."

Than looked up at his wife's face and saw the tears brimming in her eyes.

"We may have no other choice," Therese admitted.

"There are always other choices," Hecate said. "In fact, choices are my expertise. You will soon be at a crossroads, Therese. You'll know the right thing to do."

Hecate squeezed Therese's hand.

"There you are!" came a voice at the lip of the grotto.

"Hip!" Jen cried.

As happy as Than was to see his brother all in one piece, the sight of him here, in their prison, weighed heavily on him.

"We just can't get a break, can we bro'?" Hip said as he moved nearer to Than.

"Hermes must be next," Hecate said. "That's how Circe's doing it. She's using death to trap us, one at a time."

***

Jen knew the gods were in some kind of trouble, but she struggled with her feelings of elation. The last time she had seen Hip had been in a dream. He'd told her he wanted to be with her

186

for as long as she lived. Even though he hadn't been a figment and had said that the dream was true, she waited now for some sign from him that he really had meant what he'd said.

She watched him speak with the other gods, holding herself back from rushing up to him and giving him a hug. She held back, waited, knowing that the gods were trying to figure something out. But while she waited, she felt more and more deflated. Maybe she wasn't as important to him as she had hoped.

Once Hecate had explained how the witch named Circe was using death to trick the gods, Hip finally looked at Jen and gave her a sort of half-sad, half-glad smile. Her heart bloomed, and her lips stretched up in a massive grin that split her face in half.

He walked over to her and said, "I'm sorry you're here."

"I'm not," she admitted.

He put his hands on her waist, and the feel of his touch made her knees go weak.

"How come I'm not falling asleep?" she asked.

"Something's happened to my powers."

She bit her lip, still battling between the mixed emotions of worry and joy.

"I promise I won't let you get hurt," he said.

"I know." She looked at his mouth.

"The other gods will find a way to rescue us."

She nodded. "Hip, I…"

Before she could finish her sentence, he covered her mouth with his, and she sank against him.

Chapter Fifteen: One By One

Hip followed Jen through the woods toward the fruit trees.

"Follow in my footsteps," she warned. "Therese's traps are everywhere."

"That's fine by me," he said. "I like the view."

He had expected her to roll her eyes but was delighted when she turned back and winked.

As they neared an orange tree, Jen said, "Take off your shirt."

"Well, aren't *you* direct?" He laughed. "Not that I'm complaining."

He pulled his shirt over his head and caught her gazing at his body.

"Are you ready for this?" he teased.

He noticed her face go red as she turned to the tree, reached up, and plucked an orange from the lowest branches. "Tie a knot so we can load it with these."

Aha. Now he got it. His shirt was to be the bag. He made a knot, tested it, and was quite satisfied when Jen lobbed an orange his way.

"Incoming," she shouted.

He looked up to see her half way up the tree. He caught the orange just as she tossed him another. This went on for several minutes—until his makeshift bag was full.

As he helped her down from the tree, she slid so perfectly into his arms that he couldn't resist holding her there and pressing himself against her.

"I meant what I said the other night in your dream," he whispered in her ear. "I want to be with you for as long as you live."

He searched her face for her reaction and was pleased to see her smiling up at him.

"I'd give up immortality to be with you," he added. At least, he thought he would. He hadn't really thought much about it and probably shouldn't have made the offer—but it's not like he could, anyway.

Before she replied, they heard a noise—a rustling and snapping of twigs. They looked toward the sound, but couldn't see anything because of the trees.

"That's just Pudding," Jen said.

"Who?" Hip brought his brows together in confusion.

"The brown mare I told you about."

Hip peered through the trees and caught sight of a flash of green.

"That's no mare," he whispered. "Hold very still."

He narrowed his eyes and held his breath, watching for the thing he'd seen. He heard the rustle before he saw anything. This time it wasn't green. This time it was a lion's head.

"Chimera," he whispered.

"What's that?"

"I doubt we can outrun her."

"Her? Who?"

"Trust me. You don't want to know."

"Should we hide in the tree?"

Chimera's snake head could easily follow them up there, but maybe not as high as the uppermost branches. Hip nodded and the two of them climbed as high as they could go.

Shoot. The bag of oranges. It was like a sign pointing to the tree.

Jen noticed, too. "You should have brought the oranges."

"It's too late now. Listen."

Hip held his breath and drew his dagger from his boot as the monster neared them. He almost fell out of the tree when a sharp shriek from Jen startled him.

"Sn-snake!"

It was a good thing only one end of Chimera was visible at the moment.

He cupped his hand over her mouth and whispered, "It's okay. Shh."

He stroked her hair, trying to calm her, but he could feel her stiffen beneath his hands, heart pounding and mouth itching to scream.

"Oh my God," she whispered into his hand. "That snake is huge."

"That's just the tail," he whispered back, and then wished he hadn't.

Jen went into full panic mode. She flailed her arms and screamed into his hand, still cupped firmly against her mouth. Chimera spotted them in the branches with all three of her heads and barreled toward them, screeching in the fullness of terror. This was not good.

Just before she reached their tree, Chimera fell, with a thud and crack, onto the hard ground, crying and wailing in pain. She must have found one of Therese's traps.

"Come on." Hip lowered himself from the tree.

Jen refused to follow, but clung stubbornly to the branches.

"She'll get you if you stay," he warned. "Come on." He didn't mention Chimera's fire-breathing talents.

Trembling like a leaf in the wind, Jen made her way to the ground and took Hip's offered hand. He returned his dagger to its sheath in his boot and slung the bag of oranges over his shoulder.

Chimera's cries and shrieks rang out through the woods as they ran back toward the falls. Hip actually started feeling sorry for the creature, but not bad enough to not get the hell out and back to safety.

"Stop!" Jen cried. "That's one of the traps!"

Hip came to an abrupt halt inches from what he now saw were the tips of pointy sticks hidden beneath the dead leaves.

"This way!" she said, and she took his hand and ran.

As they rounded the corner near the smaller waterfall, Hip spotted Hermes.

"What the devil is going on?" Hermes asked.

***

Than had sided with Hecate and Therese about going to check on Chimera, but Hermes had a good point that it was easy to insist on the excursion when you were paralyzed and unable to go.

"We can't leave her there," Therese had said. "Not without knowing why she's here."

Hecate had agreed. "She could be a prisoner just like us."

"There's no way I'm going back," Jen had put in.

"No one expects you to," Hip had assured her. "You stay here with Than and Therese."

Hermes had reluctantly agreed to go, but only because he was obviously in love with Hecate, and Hecate was going with or without him.

Therese stirred Thanatos from his thoughts. "I can't believe what Hermes said about no one dying."

"At least my father finally caught on," Than said.

"So nobody can die?" Jen asked. "A person could fall from a high building and splat in the middle of the street and not die?"

"I'm afraid so," Than said.

"But that's a good thing," Jen argued. "Isn't it?"

"Would you want to live with a crushed skull and guts pouring out onto the street?" Therese asked.

Jen snapped her mouth shut and shook her head.

"I wonder what Circe's next move will be now that her death trap is out," Than mused.

"Oh, no," Therese said with a shaky voice.

Jen put a hand on Therese's shoulder. "Are you okay?"

"Therese, what's wrong?" Than lifted his head as far as he could.

"I think my water just broke."

All the air left Than's body as he stared at her in shock. Not here. Not in this dismal place.

"What do we do?" Jen asked. "*I* can't deliver your babies."

"Calm down." Therese maneuvered over to Than's side and lay down beside him. "It's going to be okay."

She gripped his hand like a vice, and to his surprise, he was able to grip hers back. But how much more helpless could a husband be than to be paralyzed beside his wife as she gave birth to his twins?

"They're coming," Therese murmured. "Whether we're ready or not."

***

194

Hip and Hecate guided Hermes through the woods, avoiding the traps.

"Over there," Hip pointed.

Ten yards away, Chimera lay on her side, panting, with all six of her eyes closed, but as Hip and the others neared, her eyes snapped open, and she shrieked.

"We haven't come to hurt you," Hecate called out.

"Then why have you come?" Chimera bellowed through her lion's mouth.

"We want to know why you're here," Hermes said as they stepped closer.

"And how," Hip added.

"Why should I tell you?" Chimera shrieked.

She was clearly frightened and unable to move.

"Because we want to help you," Hecate said.

"But we need to know we can trust you," Hip said.

"Can we?" Hermes asked.

Chimera panted and said nothing. Then she asked. "How do I know I can trust you?"

"You don't have many options," Hermes pointed out.

As they reached Chimera's side, Hip noticed that one of the sticks had impaled her chest just below her lion's head and blood was pouring from her body.

"If you promise not to try to kill us, we'll help you," Hecate said gently. "Come on guys. Give me a hand."

The three of them lifted Chimera up from the bed of sharpened sticks—the spear in her chest so deep that it remained lodged there. They laid her on a bed of leaves a few yards away. Then Hermes grabbed the spear and pulled it from her heart. Chimera thrashed wildly and screamed a blood-curdling scream.

Hermes removed his shirt and gave it to Hecate to press against the open wound. The corners of Hip's mouth twitched when he noticed Hecate give his cousin a once over.

"Are you hurt anywhere else?" Hecate asked Chimera.

"I can't tell. Everything hurts. I think I'm going to be sick."

"Maybe some cold water from the falls would numb her pain," Hecate said.

"What do you suggest we do?" Hermes asked. "We don't have a vessel."

"We'll have to carry her to the water," Hecate replied.

Hip and Hermes exchanged looks.

"She weighs a ton," Hermes said. "In case you haven't noticed, we've lost our strength."

"Just leave me here," Chimera said.

"If you can get on your feet, we can help you walk," Hecate said. "Can you try?"

"We need answers first," Hermes said.

"That can wait," Hecate snapped. "Are you going to help me or not?"

Hip crossed his arms. "You have to remember that I just had my head lobbed off because of her lot!"

"Yeah. I know what that's like," Hermes muttered with a wince.

"*My* lot? *My* lot?" Chimera cried. "I had nothing to do with that!"

"Didn't you help abduct Amphitrite and steal the trident?" Hip demanded.

"Yes, but…"

"Then yes, *your* lot!" he shouted.

Chimera wailed another blood-curdling scream. Hip covered his ears and looked at her, still full of angry indignation, and yet he felt accosted by her suffering and wanted it to end.

"Just kill me then!" Chimera cried, as though reading his mind.

"We can't," Hermes said. "There's no death."

Chimera wailed again.

"Come on," Hecate said. "She'll be able to tell us more if we can ease her suffering."

The three of them moved to a different part of Chimera's body—Hecate at the lion's head, Hermes in the middle with the goat's head, and Hip at the back, holding up the thick, heavy serpent. Chimera was far from steady on her four feet as she stumbled along. They made slow progress, all panting and sweating from exhaustion. Hip realized he might not like being a mortal after all. He missed his strength and stamina.

197

When they finally reached the smaller of the two waterfalls, they helped Chimera into the cold water of the shallow stream. It seemed to bring her some relief.

"Why are you helping me?" she asked them.

"Because we need some answers," Hecate said, surprising Hip. "We need the truth. As long as you are honest with us, we will continue to help you."

Chimera took a heavy breath. "You won't want to help me after you hear what I have to say."

"Let us be the judge of that," Hecate said.

Chimera spoke from her lion's head. "Circe is deranged."

"That's not news," Hermes said.

"The black magic has gone to her head," Chimera explained, as she sat in the water, panting. "My family and I thought she meant to restore power to the Titans, but apparently she has no intention of freeing them from Tartarus."

"Then what *does* she want?" Hip asked.

"We can't figure it out," Chimera said. "My father was promised the trident, but now he doubts she ever intended to give it to him."

"Did she say why she sent you here?" Hecate asked.

"She wants us all to battle it out," Chimera said. "The last few standing will get their powers and strength partially restored and become her servants on Mount Olympus."

Hip thought immediately of Jen as his mouth fell open. "And what happens to the rest?"

"They remain here," Chimera said. "Forever."

***

"I'll go get the others!" Jen said, not knowing what else to do.

"Don't leave me here!" Therese begged her. "Jen, I'm scared."

Jen watched in horror as Therese grit her teeth and grunted. Another contraction seemed to be coming on. They were happening more frequently.

"Okay, okay," Jen said. "I'm not going anywhere. Do you need water or anything?"

"Will you just, oh, just, hold on!" Therese screamed. "Stop talking!"

Jen clamped her mouth shut. Geez! She was only trying to help.

"Take this blanket," Than said. "Let some fresh water soak part of it. Then bring it back and put it on her head."

That was actually a good idea, Jen thought. At least it gave her something to do. She took the blue cotton blanket with the birds embroidered on it and held a corner of it beneath the falls. The water was freezing as it crept up her wrists and onto her sleeves. She wrung most of the water out and carried the blanket back to Therese, who was sweating and panting like a fish out of water. Jen put the corner of wet blanket across Therese's forehead.

"Hold my hand," Therese insisted.

Jen did as she said.

"Don't break it," Jen said, wincing from her friend's tight grip.

"Oh hell, oh hell, here it comes again!" Therese screamed.

"Breathe, Baby," Than said.

"Oh, I can't take this! I can't take it! Make it stop!" Therese screamed at the top of her lungs.

"You can do this." Jen moved Therese's sweaty hair from her eyes. "I know you can. You're the bravest person I know."

Jen was shocked when Therese broke into tears and cried, "I'm not brave! I want to be, but I'm not!"

Then the pain seemed to subside, because Therese relaxed, at least for the moment.

"You are brave, Baby," Than said. "I've seen it. Jen's right. You can do this."

"Okay," Therese said. "Okay. I can do this. I can. Oh, God. Oh, hell. Here it comes again!"

Just as Jen thought her hand was crushed for good, she was relieved to see the other gods had finally made it back.

"Is she…" Hecate lost her words as Jen nodded.

"Do you know what to do?" Jen asked.

Hip and Hermes exchanged worried glances, but Hecate rushed over and pulled down Therese's underpants.

"Give me that blanket," Hecate said. "I can already see a head."

Jen handed the blanket to the goddess and felt Therese's grip tighten.

"Here it comes!" Therese shouted.

"Go ahead and push, Therese," Hecate said. "As the contraction comes on, bear down."

"Oh hell! Oh holy hell!" Therese cried.

"You're doing fine," Hecate said calmly. "The baby's coming."

Jen sat up on her knees and watched with utter amazement as the baby slid like a wet baby seal out from between Therese's legs. Then she watched in horror as Hecate used a dagger to cut the umbilical cord.

"It's Hestia!" Hip said. "She's beautiful!"

The baby girl wailed, and all but Therese laughed.

"Rip that blanket in half for me, Hermes," Hecate ordered.

Hermes did as he was told.

"Oh hell, oh, God, oh, here it comes again!" Therese screamed.

Hecate handed baby Hestia off to Hermes as Jen endured another hand-crushing squeeze from Therese.

"Oh, no," Hecate said. "Don't push, Therese. Do you hear me? The boy is breech."

"What does that mean?" Jen glanced at Than, who lay on the floor with his eyes tightly shut.

"It means he's upside down," Hecate said.

Than opened his eyes. "Why is that bad?"

"The legs don't come through as easily as the head," Hecate explained. "Just wait a minute while I try to turn him."

As Hecate put a hand inside on the unborn baby, Therese screamed and writhed in pain.

"Never mind! Okay!" Hecate said. "It's okay. Let me just try to get his little feet."

"Here it comes again!" Therese screamed. "Oh hell, oh man, oh help me, please!"

"Don't push!" Hecate shouted. "Jen, I need you here!"

"What can *I* do?" Jen asked, scared to death.

"Get over here," Hecate said. "Hip, go hold Therese's hand."

Jen and Hip glanced fearfully at one another as Jen crouched beside Hecate at Therese's bent knees. Jen was horrified by the bloody mess on the ground.

"What is that?" she muttered.

"That's just the placenta," Hecate said. "Hestia's placenta. It's normal. Now reach over here and grab this tiny foot."

Jen's eyes widened in shock. She had to stick her fingers into the bloody mess? She thought she might faint as sweat broke out on her forehead. She reminded herself that she had to stay focused for her friend. Therese and her baby were on the line.

"Got it," Jen said when she finally found the foot and curled her fingers around it.

"We need to turn him so I can get to the other leg," Hecate said as Therese began to wail again.

"It's okay, Baby," Than said.

Tears sprang to Jen's eyes as she watched Hecate thrust her hand inside of Therese, cupping the baby.

"I've got it," Hecate said. "Now, Therese. Go ahead and push."

This baby did not slide out like a wet seal, Jen observed. She and Hecate had to ease him out, helping each little arm, one at a time, and then the chin. But at last the baby was free and crying just like his sister.

The entire room, save Therese, shouted their hoorays and bravos and well dones, but when Jen looked back down at her friend, she gasped. Therese was out cold.

***

When Therese woke up and saw her husband sitting up against the wall of the grotto holding a baby, she immediately suspected she was dreaming. But if they were still trapped in Circe's battlefield—Hip included—a dream was impossible. That meant her husband really *was* sitting up, and he really *was* holding one of their babies. But had both made it out alive?

She glanced around the cavern.

"You're awake," Than said, smiling down at her.

Jen sat near Therese's feet holding the other one. Therese sighed with relief as Jen smiled at her.

"Are you ready to meet your babies?" Jen asked.

Hecate turned from where she'd been washing her tunic in the falls. "They need to eat."

Therese blinked and tried to sit up, ignoring the soreness between her legs. Hecate reached over and helped her lean against the wall beside Than.

"Can you walk?" she asked him.

"Not yet. But soon. I can feel it."

"Where are Hip and Hermes?" Therese asked, noticing the other gods were missing.

"Looking for food," Jen said. "We noticed pecans and walnuts during our last outing. A nice change from all the fruit."

Anxious to hold her babies, Therese peered into the eyes of the little bundle in Than's arms.

"This is Hermes, our son," he said, gently. "And he's really hungry. He's been sucking on my finger for hours."

Therese took the baby boy into her own arms and, with Hecate's help, was able to feed him. Little Hestia was soon crying for her turn. It took some getting used to, but Therese finally got the hang of nursing. After the babies had been burped, she and Than sat side by side, each with a babe in their arms.

She was amazed by how much love she had for them, and how much she adored their sweet little bodies. Hestia had little red wisps of soft, feathery hair all over the top of her head and the roundest little bunched-up cheeks. Hermes had dark hair—almost black, like his father's, but not very much. His lips were fuller, and presently in the cutest pout. Their eyes were the darkest blue she'd ever seen. She couldn't stop gazing at her babies, stroking them, holding them ever so close. Giving them up to her aunt and uncle seemed like an impossibility to her now.

"I can't believe I'm actually getting this opportunity to hold them," Than said. "I'm almost glad we got trapped here."

Tears pricked Therese's eyes, and a sob caught in her throat, but she managed to say, "I know."

"Maybe it wouldn't be so bad to stay here."

Therese looked up at him with surprise. "You can't be serious."

"Why not?" He looked every bit as serious as he sounded.

"Well, because, first of all, we'd never see our families," she said.

"If we have to choose between our parents and our babies, it's an easy choice," he said.

"We're at the witch's mercy here," Therese complained. "We don't know what she'll do to us next."

"That's true no matter where we go," Than insisted. "We're always at the mercy of forces outside of our control."

"But what about their destiny?" Therese asked. "How can they restore faith to humanity if they're trapped in here with us?"

"If it's their fate, then it will happen," he said. "I don't know how, but it will."

Therese couldn't believe what Than was saying. As much as she wanted to live with him and their babies, she couldn't turn her back on their families and their responsibilities. A simple life didn't sound bad at all, but the entire world could be at stake.

"What if the rest of the world needs us?" she asked. "What if the other gods are in trouble?"

Than was silent for a moment. "I know we can't really live here," he finally said. "I know it's not possible. I just like thinking about it."

Therese's breath caught, and she leaned over and kissed her husband's cheek. Then she leaned down and kissed the baby girl in his arms as she tightened her hold on baby Hermes. She hated not knowing the future of her little family.

"What's not possible?" Hip asked, as he surfaced from the canyon with his shirt full of nuts.

Than told his brother what he'd been telling Therese.

"Sounds nice," Hip agreed. "I was just imagining the same for me and Jen."

"What a happy little family we could all make," Therese said to little Hermes. "Oh, what a sweet dream, Hypnos. But Than and I need to think about what we're really going to do."

"You mean if we ever get out of here?" Hermes asked as he emerged from the canyon below.

"Don't talk like that," Hecate said as she carried the newly rinsed diapers she had made from strips of the blue cotton blanket. "It does no good to think the worst."

"Oh, I'm thinking the worst, all right," Hermes said. "Take a look who I found."

Hermes held out his hand to someone below, and in the next moment, Callisto appeared.

"Callisto?" Hecate asked, bewildered.

"Not just me," the nymph said. "Marvin is here, too—down below in the canyon."

"Who's Marvin?" Jen asked.

"Apollo's lover," Hecate replied.

"You know what this means," Hermes said. "Circe has upped her game. I'd bet all the drachmas in the world on who shows up here next."

Chapter Sixteen: New Arrivals

Thanatos dived into the cool water, in what had come to be called Poseidon's River, glad to finally have a bath.

"Aren't you coming in?" he called to Hip, who sat in the shallows where the water met the bank.

"No, thanks. I'm happy right here."

Than laughed at the sight of his brother bending over to dip in his head and rinse out his hair. It gave him a flashback of the days when they were boys and their mother bathed them in one of the pools formed where the Cocytus River met the Acheron. Hip never did like baths. The memories made Than think of his own twins and how he wished he could be around to help them grow up.

"It's a lot nicer out here," Than said.

"I beg to differ."

Unused to holding his breath, Than caught water in his lungs and hacked it out. Hip was up on his feet in an instant.

"You drowning?"

Than was surprised by his brother's diligence. "I'm good."

Hip sat back in the water. "You don't sound good."

"Still getting used to not having my powers."

"Yeah. Sucks, doesn't it?"

Than lay on his back, floating, squinting against the sun. "Not when you've been paralyzed for weeks."

"Two weeks. That's nothing."

"It felt long enough."

Hip leaned back on his elbows, half in and half out of the river. The sun shone on his brilliant skin, which glowed despite the loss of his godly sheen. Than swam over to him and sat beside him, elbows back, too, soaking in the sun.

"It's not so bad here, is it?" Hip commented.

"Could be worse," Than agreed. "But I can't stop worrying about what's happening on the outside."

"Yeah. Let's not talk about it."

"Those reports from Artemis and Apollo are unsettling."

"That's an understatement."

"I feel so helpless, even now that I'm not paralyzed. It's like I'm still paralyzed, you know?"

"You have to try harder not to think about it," Hip said. "It does no good."

"Maybe not."

"You always have been the bigger worrier of the two of us."

Than grinned. "I suppose that's true."

After a while, Hip asked, "Why *couldn't* we stay here? Like you were saying the other day? Jen and I could help you raise the twins. It could be nice."

"You know the answer to that," Than replied, though the fantasy hadn't lingered far from his mind.

"Remind me."

"We can't turn our backs on the rest of the world. You heard what Apollo and Artemis said. Mount Olympus is occupied, and the gods are held up in the Underworld and at Poseidon's palace. Then there's Circe's army of zombies wreaking havoc in the upperworld. All those mortals, unable to die, and yet enslaved to do her bidding."

"But if we have no choice, and we're *forced* to stay here, it wouldn't be so bad, would it?"

Than gave his brother a sideways glance. "I suppose not, if you can forget about everyone else."

At that moment, a tremendous shriek filled the air. Than and Hip looked out toward the sound, toward the middle of the river, where the water was suddenly churning in a gigantic whirlpool. Than and Hip climbed out of the river and stepped back on the bank, watching with curious fascination and horror.

"What is that?" Hip muttered.

Than said nothing as he watched an enormous thing emerge from the water's depths and into the air, gasping and screeching and flailing about.

It was Scylla.

***

Back at the grotto, where Jen was shelling pecans and Hecate was washing rags, Hip was shocked to learn that Scylla wasn't the only new arrival to the battlefield. Apollo and Artemis had been out exploring the pink granite peaks on the opposite side of the platform, where they had come upon Echidna and Ladon.

"Circe's forcing the monsters to fight us," Artemis explained with her hands on her hips. "To prove they're worthy to rule with her on Mount Olympus."

Callisto wrapped an arm around Artemis's elbow. "Oh, no."

Hip crossed the grotto and sat beside Jen, encircling her waist and doing his best to reassure her.

"Hey," he whispered. "It's going to be okay."

Jen nodded as she continued to peel the pecans.

"That's crazy," Therese said from where she sat against the cavern wall, holding both of her babies, one in each arm. "She's just using them for her own deranged pleasure." She spoke softly, so as not to wake the babies, but her tone was far from gentle.

"That's the witch for you," Hermes said. "She's always been a little off."

"Why would Scylla fight for Circe, if she's transformed her back into a monster?" Therese asked.

"Maybe she's promised to return her back again," Than said.

"The bottom line is that these monsters are cooperating with one another to attack and destroy us," Apollo said.

"Even Chimera?" Hip asked.

"Even Chimera," Artemis said. "She's still weak, but much improved. I don't think she feels she has a choice."

"Do we?" Marvin, Apollo's lover—a tall, thin blonde in his thirties—asked. "Have a choice, I mean?"

"Circe has convinced them that either the monsters or the Olympians will make it out of this prison," Apollo said. "Not both."

Artemis added, "Meanwhile, she's amassed her armies of undead mortals…"

"But you never told us how," Than said. "How is she controlling the zombies?"

"If they cooperate," Artemis said, "they're numbed from their pain. And if they don't, they writhe in agony."

"Even the goodhearted mortals eventually give up," Apollo explained.

Hip felt Jen shudder against him.

"I'll protect you," he whispered in her ear. "I promise."

"For someone who's lost her mind, Circe's thought of everything," Hermes said.

"What are the other gods doing?" Marvin asked.

"Defending the last two realms—the Underworld and Poseidon's palace," Artemis replied. "We would have stayed and fought, too, but…" Artemis looked at Callisto as her voice trailed off.

"We need a plan," Hecate said.

"That's why we're here," Ares said as he reached the lip of the grotto, surprising them all. He held out his arm and pulled up Athena.

"We're ready for battle," Athena said in full armor with her spear and shield.

Hip had never been happier to see the gods of war.

***

As Therese and Than changed their babies' diapers and snuggled them in freshly washed and dried blanket scraps, Therese listened to Ares and Athena's reports of what was going on outside of Circe's battlefield.

"Circe has taken over the Cyclopes," Athena said. "All but Polyphemus, who is holed up in his cave."

"They're building an arsenal of lightning bolts for her," Ares explained. "That's how she was able to take over Mount Olympus."

"If it weren't for the trident and the helm," Apollo said, "the Underworld and Poseidon's palace wouldn't have a chance."

Therese noticed Ares and Athena exchange worried looks.

"Oh, no," Therese gasped. She picked up Hestia and moved closer to Thanatos. "What else has happened?"

"Poseidon's palace was breached," Ares said. "Right after Artemis and Apollo left us. Circe now controls the skies, the seas, and the land."

"The rest of the Olympians have retreated to the Underworld," Athena added. "Which is exactly where Circe seems to want them."

"If she's already controlling the undead on earth, she's pretty much got a hand in everything," Than pointed out as he held baby Hermes in his arms.

"Then why are you here?" Hermes asked Ares and Athena. "Instead of defending the other Olympians?"

Athena crossed her arms. "When we heard what Circe was planning to do—to pit the monsters against you here—we decided to follow them here."

"I followed Scylla" Ares said. "Athena followed Echidna."

"We thought if we could see the way in, we might be able to figure a way out," Athena added. "And then we'd have all of your help in the final battles."

"I'm not sure how we would have fared without you," Hip said. "We don't have the ability to call on our swords, and the only weapon I had on me when I got here was this dagger I carry in my boot."

Luckily, Therese had her bow and arrows, as did Apollo and Artemis, who, like her, never went anywhere without them. And because Than had already called upon his sword before he'd been struck with the lightning bolt, his had come over with him. But Hecate and Hermes, who, like Hip, had been tricked with death, had nothing.

"Did you?" Artemis asked. "Figure a way out?"

Athena crossed the room and started pacing. "Echidna and Ares came in at the pink granite peaks. Scylla and I came in at the river. We believe there are seams there—portals of some kind."

"Than and I entered here, though," Therese said.

"And I came in at the fruit trees," Jen added.

"The four cardinal points," Hecate said. "That makes sense. Black magic often relies on the four cardinal points."

"North, south, east, and west," Apollo murmured.

"Can you see anything?" Hermes asked him.

Apollo frowned. "I'm getting something, but I can't tell what."

"So what are we supposed to do?" Hip asked. "Go out through these seams?"

"Exactly," Athena said. "We have to pinpoint the location of at least one of them."

"But how do we open the seam?" Than asked. "We're all without our powers."

"We'll have to wait until someone enters," Ares said. "Whether it's a monster or a god."

"Then what?" Artemis asked. "We all just jump out?"

"We were thinking we should make rope," Athena said. "I can weave it out of all kinds of natural materials found here."

Ares lifted his palms. "And so we all hold onto the rope. And when the seam opens, we thrust ourselves out. Our united momentum might be enough."

Therese wrinkled her nose. It wasn't the most solid plan.

"We thought about making a fire and burning the place down," Apollo said, "but we weren't sure it would do any good."

"It could just destroy our food supply and nothing else," Artemis added. "At least your idea has no negative consequences."

"How long will it take to make a rope?" Hermes asked.

"Well, there are twelve of us, not counting the babies." Athena seemed to be doing math in the air. "At least three feet per person. Gathering materials and weaving thirty-six feet. Hmm. I would say three days."

"But here's the bigger problem," Ares said. "Before we can even attempt to make this plan of escape work, we have to incapacitate the monsters. Otherwise, they'll impede our every effort."

"What if we explain to them what we're trying to do?" Therese asked. "Wouldn't they want to help us?"

"No," Apollo said. "They want to prove they're worthy to reign with Circe on Mount Olympus. We can't count on their support."

"They've always resented the Olympians, Therese," Athena explained. "Ever since Zeus's uprising against the Titans."

"So first things first," Ares said. "We need a battle plan. We have to injure the monsters and render them helpless before we can make our escape. Is everybody on board with that?"

Therese watched breathlessly as Ares glanced around the room at each member of their solemn group. Each person who met his eyes nodded. When Ares finally glanced at her, she did the same. They had no choice. They had to injure the monsters before the monsters attacked them, and they had to do it quickly, before the last of the Olympians were defeated by Circe and her motley crew.

Therese moved to Than's side, fighting tears. What was the world coming to, just as their precious babies had entered it?

***

Jen held both babies in her arms and paced around the grotto, bouncing as she walked, to keep the twins sleeping. She stayed out of the way of the gods, who were inspecting their gear— sheathing and unsheathing swords, tightening bow strings, inspecting arrows, and sharpening daggers on the rocks of the grotto. Therese was among them, which scared Jen to death.

"Are you sure you should go?" Jen asked her in a low voice, so as not to draw attention from the others. "Are you sure you're up to this? You did just have, not one, but two babies."

217

"I'm sure," Therese said.

"Quit worrying," Hip intervened. "You've never seen her in battle. She's a sharp shooter."

Hip winked at Therese, who smiled back, but this brought Jen little reassurance.

"She's the only one who can feed them," Jen pointed out. "What if they get hungry?"

"If they won't suck on your finger, then give them an orange or an apple slice to suckle," Therese said. "I don't plan to be away long. I'll do my part and hurry back."

Jen had a bad feeling about all of this. The first week here had been a godsend. She had begun to fantasize about staying with Hip and Therese at this place forever. But she supposed all good things must come to an end, and this one had—that was for sure.

Taking care of two defenseless babies was not the least of her worries, either. She decided she would not be having children of her own. Not only was the birth horrendously painful-looking, but dealing with the minute-to-minute needs of them once they were born was exhausting. She wasn't sure why any mother ever went through a second pregnancy.

"But none of you have your powers," Jen objected. "I may as well be going, too." She couldn't really see why the least experienced at taking care of babies would be the one left behind to do it.

Hip pushed her hair from her eyes and wrapped a strand behind her ear, kissing her softly on the forehead. "You and Marvin have no experience fighting monsters. You'll help us more here, caring for the babies."

"Can't you stay, too?" she asked him, already knowing the answer.

He kissed her on the lips. "I'll be back soon."

"I need you to keep the babies safely hidden," Therese said. "I'm counting on you."

Jen wasn't so sure who had the harder job, and as the babies squirmed awake in her arms, about to make their next demands, she thought she'd much rather be battling monsters.

Chapter Seventeen: Let the Battle Begin

Therese searched for the next foothold along the canyon wall as she followed Apollo and Artemis up to the platform, where the Olympians had watched her fight McAdams four years ago. Callisto wasn't far below, taking up the rear. Therese never thought she'd see this place again, much less fight another battle here. The memory of Hades thrusting her sword into the helpless body of McAdams made her shiver.

Her belly was still sore, and her breasts were tender, but she grabbed the furthest rock she could reach and pulled herself up. She and the other gods didn't have the luxury of taking their time. They needed to incapacitate the monsters, build their rope, and get the hell out.

Not that things on the outside would be any less dangerous. In fact, even though she agreed one hundred percent with Ares and Athena's plan, she worried her babies would be in more danger out there than they were in here. If the Underworld was the last stronghold of the Olympians, and if zombies were terrorizing the mortals, where on earth could she take her children to safety?

When they had at last reached the summit, she ran to her position, looking out over Poseidon's river from one of the longer sides of the oblong platform. Artemis stood with her back to Therese about twenty feet away keeping watch over Demeter's woods. These two areas—the river and the woods—

covered more ground than the rocky caverns on both ends of what was shaped like a racetrack. Apollo was positioned north of them and was scanning the pink granite peaks. All three had their arrows fit and bows drawn, ready to strike.

Callisto had no bow or arrow, but she did have a spear, which she often used for hunting in the woods with Artemis back home, and she stood looking out over the grotto and the deeper canyon, keeping watch for possible invaders. It had been hard for Therese to relinquish that job to the nymph, to not be able to keep her own eyes on the place where her babies were hidden, but she knew she was needed for her skills with the bow where Scylla was most likely to be.

Therese could see another of their three teams getting ready at Poseidon's river, where they planned to cull out Scylla. That team consisted of their strongest swimmers, aside from her: Ares, Hecate, and Thanatos. The remaining gods—Athena, Hypnos, and Hermes—had gone to Demeter's woods to hunt any monsters that might be hiding there. If Artemis could get a visual, she'd shoot.

It was possible that the monsters were all in one location, making plans to attack the gods. If that was the case, the most likely meeting place was the river, since Scylla's ability to navigate over land was limited.

Therese believed the other monsters, not having gills, would prefer land. She imagined Echidna, Chimera, and Ladon had taken to Demeter's woods, where there was ample food.

221

Apollo had disagreed with her speculation and was sure the serpents were more likely to have set up camp in the granite mountains, where they could maneuver more easily over smooth rock. He believed the caverns and crevices offered safer hiding places than the woods, which were set with Therese's old traps and had already harmed Chimera.

Eventually both of the other teams would end up there, at the granite mountains, if they found no monsters in the woods or the river. The plan was to incapacitate the monsters and then retreat. Simple enough, right?

Therese chewed on her bottom lip as she watched Thanatos dive into the river, with Ares and Hecate on either side. They started south, near the falls, and would swim the length of the river—about a hundred yards—toward the granite peaks. She chewed and chewed, even after she drew blood. She held her breath and waited.

***

Hypnos and Hermes guided Athena past the traps in Demeter's woods. Fortunately, they weren't trying to be quiet. Hermes and Athena might have a knack for stealth, but Hip had never needed to develop one.

Taunting, however, was something Hip could do—and he could do it well. Everyone who had ever known him would probably vouch for that.

"Oh, I doubt we need to worry about Chimera," Hypnos said in a loud, arrogant voice. "She's probably off licking her wound. And Echidna doesn't have the balls to attack us. She's used to hiding behind her mommy and daddy."

Hip froze at the snap of a twig—they all did. When they heard no more, they glanced around the trees. Finally they continued walking.

"What about Ladon?" Athena asked. "He does have a hundred heads."

"No worries," Hermes said. "He couldn't be less bright."

Hip heard another snap. Now he was sure someone was in the woods, but whether it was Pudding, the brown mare, or something else, he didn't know.

"Tsk, tsk. What a shame," Hip said. "To have all those heads and not one brain."

Athena and Hermes laughed.

"You're funny *and* poetic," Hermes said.

From the branches above them, a huge, green serpent's head darted down and wrapped its neck around Hip's waist. Athena was fast with her sword, slicing the neck in half. But other heads descended down upon them. Hip drew his dagger and went to work, his heart pumping with fear and excitement. Hermes used Athena's spear. The last thing any of them needed was to become incapacitated without their godly abilities of quick healing. After three of Ladon's necks had been sliced completely through, the entire beast writhed in pain, shrieking as parts of his great serpent body began to fall from the branches. Hip jumped out of the way, barely missing being squashed. Then, one by one, like angry birds, arrows flew from the platform and lodged themselves in the thick green skin of the beast. Hip and his companions backed away as the enormous serpent finally fell, defeated, on the ground.

Before they had time to move on, Athena gasped.

Hip spun toward her, but not in time to stop the spear that was put through her waist by Chimera.

"Who's laughing now?" the monster roared with her lion's head.

Hip had known he would come to regret carrying that beast to heal. They should have left her to suffer.

As Athena collapsed on the ground beside Ladon, Hermes ran after Chimera. He wouldn't have caught up to her had she not tripped on a vine and fallen, lion's head first, onto the ground. Before she could clamber to her feet, Artemis's arrows came once again, like automatic artillery, one after another into Chimera's flesh. Hermes took up Athena's spear and impaled the eye of the goat's head for good measure.

"That's for Athena!" he growled as he pulled the spear back out.

Hip had remained guarding Athena, who lay on her back, still and pale, on bloody leaves, the spear sticking up through her belly between the breast plate and girdle of her armor.

Hermes turned her body over, gently, so he could see the back of the spear. It was one of Therese's sticks, sharpened at both ends, no doubt dug up from the ground by Chimera. Hermes laid Athena back down, and without any warning, grasped the spear and pulled it from her gut in one quick sweep.

Athena shrieked and then was still and quiet again, her gray eyes open, her face pale.

"Let's get her to the stream," Hip said.

In a barely audible voice, Athena murmured, "Complete the mission."

"We can't leave you here," Hermes argued.

"Hide me and go," she ordered. "Come back for me later."

Hypnos pulled off his shirt, wadded it up, and pressed it against her wound. "Hermes will go. I'll stay. There's no telling what those beasts would do if they discovered you."

    ***

Thanatos searched the waters high and low for Scylla as he swam in line with Ares and Hecate down the river. Without his godly vision, he was unable to see more than twenty feet in front of him, even though the water was clear and filled with very few fish and plant life. It was exhausting, for the water ran from the bigger waterfall near the grotto all the way to the granite mountains for a hundred yards, and he was constantly having to lift up his head for air. There wasn't much of a current to help him along, either. He sincerely doubted Scylla could stand to be anywhere else, though, especially after he had watched Therese attempt to maneuver in the beast's body. Water was the only logical place for Scylla to be.

And yet, here they were, nearing the end of the river, where it hit up against the pink granite banks, and they'd seen no sign of her.

When he emerged from the river onto the banks, gasping for breath, he heard a sharp scream from the platform. He turned to see Therese running at her top speed from her post toward Callisto. The scream came again. It was Callisto. Something was wrong at the grotto!

Thanatos climbed from the river and scrambled along the bank back toward the falls. Ares and Hecate were right on his heels. He kept glancing up at the platform, expecting Therese to glance down at him as she ran parallel to him, but she never did, not once. She was singular in her focus, precise and driven in her stride. She reached Callisto while Than still had fifty more yards to go. He expected to see Therese fit an arrow and draw her bow, aimed at whatever monster must be waiting for him just around the bend, but, instead, Therese dropped her weapons and fell to her knees.

***

Jen knew it did no good to keep watch on the edge of the grotto, especially when she risked being seen, but she couldn't help it. She had to know what was going on.

"What do you see?" Marvin asked from where he sat with baby Hermes, who'd been restless and fussy and wearing Jen out.

"Nothing. Just Callisto on the platform."

Hestia gurgled from her makeshift bed on the cavern floor.

"Uh-oh," Marvin sighed. "Guess who's waking up."

"That wasn't much of a nap, was it?" Jen said without inflection.

"They can probably sense our anxiety," Marvin mused.

Jen lifted her arms in the air and then dropped them. "Well, I don't know what to do about that."

"Maybe we should sing."

Jen resisted rolling her eyes as she waited to see if Hestia might fall back to sleep, but instead, the baby pinched up her face and took a deep breath just before she began to wail.

"Lord, not again." Jen took the baby in her arms and paced.

She was surprised when Marvin started humming—not by the fact that he was humming, but by how beautiful his voice was. Hestia stopped squirming and opened her blue eyes, listening.

Jen turned a smile of astonishment to Marvin. "It's working."

She had to admit that his voice was amazing, and something about it began to calm her, too. She sat against the wall of the cave across from him and allowed herself to relax to the sound of his voice.

Suddenly Marvin stopped and his jaw dropped open. Jen followed his gaze to the opening of the grotto. A dark-haired woman with turquoise eyes peered over the cliff edge below the falls and smiled at them. The water streamed down her hair and face like water from a shower head. She must be a goddess, Jen thought.

"Don't stop," the woman said. "Your voice is lovely."

"Who are you?" Marvin asked.

"I should ask the same of you," the woman replied. "You are apparently mortals and friends of the gods?"

"Yes," Jen said, bouncing Hestia, who'd begun to whimper. "I'm Jen and that's Marvin. And you are?"

"What a lovely little family you make," the woman said.

Jen scoffed. "It's not what you think. These babies aren't mine. Thank God."

Marvin climbed to his feet, blushing and shaking his head. The guy was in his thirties. How could this woman think they were together?

"My mistake." The woman smiled—a little too big, in Jen's opinion.

"So which goddess are you?" Marvin asked. "Aphrodite?"

It was the woman's turn to blush. "How sweet. I like you already, Marvin."

Jen climbed to her feet, too, beginning to feel uneasy over this woman's reluctance to reveal her name.

"May I?" the woman pointed to baby Hestia.

Jen gripped the baby protectively against her. "She's a bit fussy right now, so maybe not."

"I'm sure I could soothe her. I've had many babies of my own."

"No offense," Jen said. "But I don't know you. So…"

"You never did tell us your name," Marvin added.

"Echidna," the woman said. "Have you heard of me?"

Jen thought the name did sound familiar, but she couldn't place it. She thought she heard the gods refer to her several times, but…wait a minute. Just as Jen began to recall who Echidna was, a serpent's tongue lashed out of the woman's mouth, like a whip, and coiled around Hestia, pulling the baby free of Jen's arms.

Jen ran toward the monster, but the serpent's tail, long and massive, with a snake's head on the end of it, jerked up from the canyon wall and swatted Jen like a fly. Her body was hurled against the back wall of the grotto. Pain radiated throughout her body, and she fell in a heap on the ground. She tried to blink, but the world was spinning, spinning, and then it was black.

Chapter Eighteen: Mercy

Hypnos dragged Athena across the dead leaves of the woods to a thicket that backed up against a large boulder. He could hear the smaller falls, so they couldn't be too far away, but he didn't want to risk taking the injured goddess out in the open without Hermes to help him fend off monsters. So he crouched on his backside, knees pulled up close, gripping Athena's sword, ready to strike. Athena lay curled on her side between him and the rock, holding his bloody shirt against her wound. She was deathly quiet.

"Are you in pain?" he whispered.

"I'm not allowing myself to think of it," she replied. "But you shouldn't remain here with me. They need you."

"Without your godly abilities to heal, these monsters could do serious damage to you."

"This is about more than me. This is about more than you." She coughed up blood, sputtered, took a breath, and then added, "This is about the world."

"I understand that, but I can't leave you." Then he added, "The world isn't here. You are."

Hip then heard a terrifying scream from the platform, and he stiffened and held his breath. The scream came again, followed by the sound of someone running toward him from the granite side of the battlefield. He gripped the sword, ready to defend Athena.

"Hypnos?" Hermes called.

Hip sprang from the thicket.

"Good," Hermes said in a low voice. "Stay with her. I'm headed to the falls."

The scream came again, ringing out over the entire woods. Hermes took off for the grotto with Athena's spear in hand. Hip wanted desperately to follow. As he crawled back into the thicket to guard the wounded goddess, all he could think of was Jen. He knew no god could hear him, but he prayed, begging and pleading for her safety. At that moment, he realized he couldn't exist without her. He'd rather die and dwell as a soul in the Elysian Fields with no memories than to ever be parted from her.

"Go," Athena said. "I know you want to."

He did want to. More than anything. "I won't leave you," he said again, gripping her sword.

***

When Therese heard Callisto's wail, she knew it could only mean one thing: the grotto was threatened. Without thinking of anything else, she ran and ran and ran. Grass may or may not have hit against her legs. The sun may or may not have shone down on her. The wind may or may not have whipped her hair against her face. She was aware of nothing but getting to Callisto.

As she reached the nymph, who screamed repeatedly with her spear lifted on the end of a shaky arm, Therese was horrified by what she saw slithering down the canyon wall opposite them. She dropped to her knees.

Echidna dangled little Hermes and Hestia over the deeper canyon and the falls below—holding them each by a foot. The babies' screams could be heard, like bleating lambs, despite the thundering falls.

"What do you want?" Therese jumped to her feet and waved her open hands above her head. "I'll do anything! Please!"

"The surrender of every god here, of course," Echidna hissed. "Can you promise me that?"

Therese glanced around at the battlefield below, for the first time aware of anything other than Echidna and her twins. To her right, she saw Hermes rounding the corner from the woods. He stopped dead in his tracks at the sight of the beast. To her left, she saw Than, followed by Ares and Hecate, rounding the corner from the river. All were immobilized by the terrifying sight of the babies dangling over the dangerous drop below.

Apollo and Artemis had now caught up to her and Callisto. She looked at them with her mouth hanging open, unsure if the gods would be willing to surrender the fate of the world in exchange for her babies. Tears streamed from her eyes and into her mouth as she searched their faces, hoping for their support. Her stomach twisted into one hell of a knot.

"Help me!" she begged.

***

Thanatos stopped when he saw the beast with his babies hanging from each of her hands over the raging falls. Hate and bile raged up to his throat, and he knew in that moment that, whatever it took, he would kill Echidna.

He heard Therese make her pleas to the monster and the monster's reply.

"We surrender!" Than shouted with his arms in the air. "You win!"

"No, we don't!" Ares growled as he hefted his spear toward Echidna, apparently forgetting his lack of godly strength.

The spear grazed her tail and fell into the water below.

Therese screamed.

Echidna slithered down the canyon wall and, with the babies curled against her breast, scurried across a cliff edge toward the smaller waterfall.

Than drew his sword and ran after her, full of rage and terror.

***

Therese scrambled down from the platform along the canyon wall. She was shaking so violently that she slid part way down and scraped the flesh from the back of her thigh. After the initial sting, she could no longer feel it, could no longer think, except to know that she had to get to her babies.

Once she reached the ground below—the lip of the deeper canyon—she took off running after Thanatos, but before she could make it very far, Scylla shot up from the water below, shrieking in terror. Therese stopped abruptly as the enormous serpentine heads flailed about, blocking her path.

Ares's spear had pierced through one of the monster's four eyes. She must have been hiding beneath the falls when he had sent his weapon for Echidna.

Therese fitted an arrow to her bow and struck Scylla at one of the dog's heads. Arrows flew from the platform above her as Apollo and Artemis followed suit. Hecate and Ares surrounded the beast, swinging their weapons. Therese glanced up to the grotto to see Marvin looking down in horror, white as a sheet. She wondered why Jen wasn't beside him. Had something happened to her?

She refused to allow herself to ponder such a possibility as she navigated around Scylla's flailing pincers down the edge of the canyon toward the smaller waterfall and Demeter's woods after Than. As she ran, she fitted an arrow, ready for combat, as Ares had taught her long ago.

***

Hip held his breath so he could better hear the distant sounds coming from the falls and the platform. Callisto's incessant, pulsing screams had his heart playing havoc with his ribcage. Then she was silent, and he heard nothing for many minutes except a dull shout here and another there—the precise words or speaker imperceptible to him. He glanced back at Athena, whose eyes were wide, as she, too, was listening. It sucked beyond measure not to have godly hearing. He wanted some sign that Jen and the others were okay.

Not long after, he heard Scylla's shrill shrieks and another outpouring of indistinguishable shouts. Or cries? The thought that the others were calling for his help seized him. Should he abandon Athena, just in case?

Before he could make up his mind over what to do, he heard something moving toward him in the woods. Athena noticed it, too. They both held still and remained silent, listening. Then the bleating of lambs seemed to fill the woods all at once.

Those weren't lambs, Hip realized. Those were the twins.

***

Than couldn't breathe. He was wild and frantic and determined as he ran past the smaller waterfall and into Demeter's woods after Echidna. He could think only of his babies, whose cries rang out in desperation. He would save them. He had to. He would do whatever it took. He ran in the direction of their wails.

"Echidna!" he shouted, burning his throat. "I'll make the others surrender! I'll do whatever you want!" Again he shouted, "Echidna!"

Think, he told himself. Focus! The beast's massive tail was his greatest threat. He could slice Echidna's arms or head off with his sword, but that tail with its serpent's head could beat him down and keep him from reaching his twins. If he was going to save them, he had to find a way to control the tail.

He stopped short and almost fell as the momentum carried him forward. One of Therese's traps from four years ago had nearly made him its victim. If he hadn't known where they were, he would have fallen and impaled himself on the dozen sticks partially hidden by the leaves in the dip in the ground. If only there was a way of herding Echidna into one of these traps.

Something barreled up behind him, and he turned, expecting another monster—Chimera perhaps—but was relieved to see Therese. She ran into his arms, her tears wetting his neck and causing his own to burst free.

She was shaking, as though it was fifty below freezing.

"We can do this," he whispered through a tight throat.

"Back off!" came Echidna's command from deeper in the woods. "Back off, or I'll strangle the boy child and keep the girl as leverage."

"Please don't!" Therese screamed. "We'll do what you want!"

"Get the other gods to agree to surrender, and I'll return at least one of these brats alive!"

Therese grabbed her stomach and doubled over with a dry heave.

"Look at me." He held her face between his hands and gazed into her eyes. "Be strong. We *will* save them."

He kissed her quickly on the mouth. Then, in one fell swoop, he wrapped his hand around one of the sharpened sticks from her old trap and pulled it from the ground.

"Can you shoot these with your bow?" he whispered.

"They won't fly with the same precision as…"

"Your target is her massive tail. I want you to nail that bitch to the trees."

***

Therese used her sword to create ridges in the backs of the sharpened sticks, so she could fit them to her bow. McAdams's dried blood covered the ends of them, but she didn't shudder or hesitate in the least at her work. Nothing mattered right now but saving her twins.

Before she had finished preparing the spears, she heard footfalls at her rear. She turned, ready to strike, only to find Apollo and Artemis approaching.

"We're here to help," Artemis said.

"Ares and the others are fighting Scylla," Apollo murmured.

"Back off!" Echidna wailed. "I will strangle this child!"

Therese whispered the plan to them, and they divided up the sticks and spread out.

"Echidna!" Than called. "Come out and let's talk."

Therese felt adrenaline coursing through her as the moment of truth advanced. This was the most important moment of her life. She couldn't imagine a time when anything more important would be hanging in the balance.

She reminded herself that her babies were destined to restore faith in humanity. They were going to live. She and the others were going to save them.

A voice inside her head asked, "But at what cost?"

She silenced the voice and crept into position.

***

The first thing Hip noticed after his brother asked Echidna to come out and talk was that he could no longer hear one of the twins.

With Athena's powerful sword gripped firmly in one hand, he crept from the thicket wishing he had more stealth, but nonetheless determined to sneak up on the beast he could hear just a few yards ahead. He weaved in and out of the trees and then went stock-still when he saw her.

From the waist up, she had the proportions of an average woman, but what gave her height and formidability was her enormous tail. Presently, it was coiled beside her, poised to strike.

At that moment, he understood the sword would do him no good. If he attempted to strike her, the tail would whip around and slam him to the ground, and there'd be no chance of saving the babies. What he needed was his dagger, and he needed to get his dagger to her throat.

He carefully laid the sword down in the leaves and slid his weapon from his boot.

***

Thanatos took careful steps in the direction of the baby's cries, his stomach in knots over the silence of the other baby, whom he could no longer hear.

Please let both babies be okay, he prayed.

Echidna spotted him at the same time as he spotted her.

"I just want to talk," he said.

"Then put down your sword."

He dropped it at his feet.

"Foolish, aren't you?"

Echidna swung her tail in a thunderous sweep, like a giant wave, right in his direction, but a barrage of spears penetrated the tail, and in some places, pinned it to the ground and to the trunks of trees.

Thanatos grabbed his sword and plunged toward her, but Echidna threw one of the babies at him in a defensive move. He dropped the sword and held out his arms, unable to breathe as he navigated over dead leaves and branches, trying not to trip. He held his breath as his precious child sailed through the air.

A vine grabbed his boot, and he fell on the hard ground just as the baby was about to hit. Than scrambled to his knees, his feet, and lurched out just in time to break the fall. Little Hestia screamed at the top of her lungs, but otherwise she seemed okay. Tears filled his eyes.

When he looked up at the monster, he couldn't believe his eyes. Hip was on her back, his dagger at her throat, but Echidna was full of hysteria and panic. She waved baby Hermes around by a leg, screaming at everyone to back away.

"Back away! Or I will dash out his brains!"

The baby made no sound.

Therese rushed up behind Than, shaking like an epileptic. He handed Hestia over to her as they watched Echidna with terror. Hip made eye contact with Than, who nodded. He wanted Hip to do it. Cut her throat, and he would catch the boy.

Than rushed toward the monster as Hip scraped the dagger across her throat and blood poured out. But instead of dropping the baby, Echidna flung him through the air. Than's heart stopped beating as he watched his son fly though the low hanging branches twenty yards away. The most intense feelings of desperation and helplessness overcame him as he ran, knowing there was no way he could catch this one, too.

A scream fled from his throat—high pitched, like a girl's. If only he had his godly powers, he could make it.

And then, miracle of miracles, from the woods, Ares ran out, his arms outstretched. Like the most skilled running back on the face of the earth, he caught the baby in the nick of time.

Thanatos had never loved Ares more.

Chapter Nineteen: Fallen Angels

The exhausted warriors left Echidna trapped in the woods and headed back to the grotto. Hypnos carried Athena. Although he was thankful and relieved that the babies were back in the arms of their parents, he had a bad feeling about Jen and wouldn't be able to share in the joy of victory displayed by the others until he saw her face and knew she was safe.

"Oh, my sweet babies!" Therese said again. "I can't thank everyone enough for your part."

"They seemed fine to you, Apollo?" Than asked

"Just hungry, which I'm sure you'll soon remedy," the god of healing replied.

"And Scylla's incapacitated?" Artemis asked Ares as they left the woods.

"Oh, yes," Ares said in an arrogant tone. "She's not going anywhere."

Hip wished it hadn't been Ares that had saved the day, because now everyone was being especially nice and grateful toward him, and he was gloating like a prancing peacock.

Hermes ran to meet them as they neared the smaller waterfall. "Let me help you there, Hypnos."

"How's Jen?" Hypnos asked.

"You'll want to brace yourself, cousin." Hermes lifted Athena into his arms with a grave expression on his face.

As soon as Hip's hands were free, he took off running. He passed Scylla, where she lay badly injured in the pool beneath the smaller falls. He scrambled up the canyon wall as fast as he could, nearly slipping on the wet rock before reaching the grotto. When he was at last on the cliff edge, he stared down in horror at Jen, laid out on the cavern floor, Hecate and Marvin bent over her.

He rushed to her side and fell to his knees. Her skull was crushed, and a pool of blood lay next to her. Her beautiful blond hair was mangled in it.

For many moments he couldn't speak as he took it all in. Her eyes were closed, and he couldn't tell if she was breathing. One of her shoulders appeared at an odd angle, as though bones were crushed there, too.

He finally mustered the ability to ask, "Is she dead?"

"No one can die, Hypnos," Hecate said gently. "At least, not right now."

"But as soon as we leave this place, as soon as my brother returns to his duties…"

Hecate gripped his hand and said, "I'm afraid so."

***

When Hypnos started running for the grotto, Therese felt a chill crawl down her spine.

"What's happened?" she asked Hermes.

"I'm afraid your friend was fatally injured," the messenger god replied.

Therese felt dizzy and her knees went weak. "That can't be," she said breathlessly, unable to think. "That can't be."

"Therese, I…" Than's voice broke off as Therese handed him Hestia and ran for the bigger falls.

Before she reached the lip of the grotto, she heard Hip's wail of sorrow ring out across the canyon. *This can't be*, she repeated to herself. She refused to believe until she saw with her own eyes.

When she did see, she still refused to believe. She knelt between Hip and Hecate with her hands over her mouth.

"This can't be," she said out loud. "She can't be dead."

"Not yet," Hecate said. "But I'm afraid... I'm so sorry, Therese."

Hecate put her arms around Therese and kissed the top of her head, but Therese could barely feel it. She was numb, and now, too, she felt deaf and blind. A dull ache pulsed in her ears. Her heart started beating very fast. She couldn't breathe.

She clutched her chest.

"Jen!" she screamed, vaguely aware that she'd caused those around her to flinch.

Hecate was saying something at her right, and Hip was saying something at her left, but all Therese could hear was the pulse of her own blood thudding in her ears where the pain was.

***

244

Thanatos held his babies close as Hermes carefully laid Athena down in the shallow part of the stream near the smaller waterfall. Apollo bent over her to inspect her wound. Than couldn't feel sorrier for his brother. He wracked his brain for ideas—ways around Jen's death. Soon they hoped to leave Circe's battlefield, and his duties would be restored to him. But how could he take the soul that was the love of his brother's life?

Therese, too, would be miserable over losing her best friend. Than could hardly think of what this would do to poor Bobby and Mrs. Holt. There had to be a way out of this. What could he do?

The babies were hungry. He had to get them up to the grotto to Therese. He was able to get Hermes and Artemis to help him while Apollo and Ares stayed behind with Athena.

Artemis climbed to the lip of the grotto. Hermes stopped halfway up. Then Thanatos passed one baby at a time up to the other two gods before climbing all the way up himself.

When he reached their little camp, he found Hip sobbing into Jen's belly and Therese curled up in a ball against the opposite wall. Marvin and Callisto looked up at Than with somber faces.

"The babies are okay?" Marvin asked.

"Just hungry," Than managed to say through a dry throat as he took the infants back from Artemis and Hecate.

245

He crossed the cavern to Therese and carefully sat on the ground beside her.

"Your babies need you," he said.

She seemed to wake up from her stupor as he handed them over to her. He helped her lift up her shirt inconspicuously and get the babies suckling, so their cries would stop rattling everyone's nerves. He covered her to protect her modesty and to keep the babies warm.

Therese held their sweet little heads to her breasts as tears rolled down her face.

"I'm going to break my oath," she said. "I want to do for Jen what you did for me."

The other gods gasped.

"Don't do it, Therese," Hecate warned. "You'll lose the trust and respect of everyone."

"Then *I'll* do it," Hip said. "I'll break my oath."

"Please," Artemis said. "Please don't even consider it. Our pantheon is already crumbling. The only thing we have left is our word to each other."

"We swore," Hermes said. "That has to mean something."

Than felt sick to his stomach. He'd started down the slippery slope that Hip and Therese now wanted to follow. Would he do it again to have Therese as his wife? Of course. But did he think Hip should follow in his footsteps? No way.

"What if you take her to Tartarus with Pete?" Therese asked Than with hope in her eyes. "If she has to die, could she stay there, so we could still talk to her?"

"You don't want that for her," Hecate said. "Eternity is a long time for boredom. She'd be miserable."

"But she'd have Pete," Therese argued. "And I'd visit her every day."

Than pushed Therese's hair away from her face, since her hands were full and she couldn't. As he tucked her fiery red hair around her ears, he said gently, "I don't control the sentencing. Only the judges decide where a soul will go."

Therese's face pinched up in disappointment as more tears flowed down her face. "Is there nothing we can do?"

"Someone could trade places with her," Hermes said. "It's the only way accepted by the Fates. Someone else would have to die in her place."

***

Hypnos knew what he had to do. He had to take Jen's place. He didn't want to exist without her, without having had the chance to love her properly. He'd rather go to the Elysian Fields.

He ran the back of his hand against her soft face, wishing she would wake up and smile at him, just one more time before he died.

As certain as he was that this was what he should do, he was terrified of mortal death. He'd never had to think about it before. Finality. The end. A cold sweat broke out on his forehead, and a panic began to rise in his throat. This was one of his last and final days in existence. He would be no more.

Glancing across the room at his brother, he thought better of telling him his intentions. Thanatos would only try to talk him out of it. He looked at Therese, holding their babies, and at his brother, helping her, and he admired what a sweet family they made, even though it was temporary. As soon as the duties of death returned, Thanatos would have to distance himself from his infants. It would be devastating.

But at least Than would be able to watch his children grow up from afar. Hypnos would die without ever experiencing marriage and fatherhood.

Yet Hip felt no envy. He felt only sadness. He loved his brother and hated to leave him.

As though in sympathy with him, the ground beneath him shuddered.

"What was that?" Callisto asked.

A few stones and a spray of dust fell from the ceiling of the grotto.

"An earthquake?" Hip asked.

The ground fell beneath them, and a crack ran along the ceiling.

"We need to bail ship," Hermes said. "I'll help you with the mortal."

Hip carefully slid his hands beneath Jen's armpits as Hermes lifted her legs. Her head bobbed at odd angles, so he lifted it to rest against his chest. He coughed at the dust falling in his face, in his mouth.

The ground shook again, and a falling rock hit Artemis on the shoulder. She staggered.

"I'm okay," she said.

"We can't climb down with her like this," Hermes said. "Throw her over your shoulder. I'll climb below you and help with the weight."

Therese and Than were fumbling with blankets, turning them into slings, but Hip feared they were taking too long.

"Come on!" he shouted to them as the ground began to open up.

They scrambled down the canyon wall as more stones slipped and fell all about them.

"To the platform!" Apollo shouted from below.

Ares had flung Athena over his shoulder in the same way Hip had Jen, and they all staggered along the quivering canyon toward the platform. When they reached the lower canyon, they looked back in horror as their grotto collapsed and the rocks began to roll down the wall and hurl through the air toward them. Hip winced when he noticed Therese fall several feet with the baby strapped across her chest.

As they scrambled along the lower canyon toward the wall leading up to the platform, another quake jerked them off their feet, but before a single one of them could recover, an explosion of rocks burst into the air, and a powerful wind railed against them. Hip was on his knees holding onto Jen for dear life, when suddenly he found himself on the rainbow steps inside the gates of Mount Olympus. All of them were there, lying on the steps: Ares with Athena, Than and Therese with their babies, Hecate and Hermes behind him, and Apollo and Artemis each holding the hands of their lovers. Hip's godly powers were immediately restored, as were those of the other gods, and prayers were assaulting him from every god he knew.

Through the great hall, Hip saw the fire from Hephaestus's forge spraying into a band of Cyclopes, who returned fire from the center of the fortress with lightning bolts. An army of gods surrounded Zeus's palace, many of whom were engaged in hand-to-hand combat with zombies empowered with Circe's black magic. Briareos created a tremendous wind surrounding the fortress, and the limbs of some of the zombies had fallen from their bodies and gotten caught up in his cyclone. As Meg and Tizzie decapitated undead soldiers, the heads were added to the awful swirl of decomposing body parts. Rhode and Amphitrite gathered some of the zombies in Poseidon's golden net, while Phobos and Deimos deflected lightning bolts with their incredible shields. Even Aphrodite and her Charities swung their swords with the other daughters and sons of the Olympians. Poseidon led them with his trident. Dangerous sparks flew in the air all about them.

Athena rejuvenated in a blaze of glory, and, together with Ares, Apollo, Artemis, and the others who had been trapped in Circe's battlefield with her, she conjured her sword and charged into battle.

Hip retreated with Jen toward the gates and immediately prayed to the Fates.

I relinquish my immortality to Jen Holt. I swear on the River Styx to take her place. Please do it now.

All the strength that had returned to his body slowly drained away.

He was vaguely aware of Therese screaming across the courtyard to him, something about his father's chariot.

When Jen lifted her face and stood on her feet, she looked at him with wide eyes. Her body glowed with the beauty reserved for the gods. She'd always been beautiful, but now she was breathtaking. Her injuries were healed. The blood was gone. Her hair blew like golden rays in the wind around her face. He drank in the vision of her, as though trying to imprint it permanently on his eyes.

"Hip?"

He took her face with his hands and pressed his lips to hers. He would kiss her as hard and as long as he could. He would kiss her until his brother came for his soul, after which he would never kiss her again.

***

Therese cupped little Hermes in her arms, who squirmed in his makeshift sling, as she stumbled back from the rainbow steps of Mount Olympus, surrounded by the chaos of war. An undead soldier headed toward her, and she elbowed him out of the way, pleased to finally have her powers restored. Than climbed to his feet behind her, holding Hestia. From somewhere beneath the helm of invisibility, Hades screamed at her through prayer to get the mortals to safety. His chariot was parked outside the gates. She was to go now.

She turned to Than, who was untying the sling and handing Hestia over. His face was pale, his expression grave.

"Take her, before she dies in my arms." He kissed Hestia's head, and then did the same to little Hermes.

She'd almost forgotten. Now that Thanatos was back to normal, he could no longer hold their babies.

Therese's heart was breaking in two, but she had to get the twins away from him.

"I'm so sorry," she said.

"Go," Than warned just before pulling her down and out of the way of a streak of lightning.

"I'm going to take Jen," Therese said. "Look. She's okay."

"Oh, no." Than's face became even graver. "Oh, hell no!"

Therese was baffled as Than disintegrated and one of him ran from her side toward Hypnos. Other versions of

Thanatos also stormed toward the palace, knocking zombies over left and right. She followed the one that headed for Hip, dodging fire.

"What have you done?" Than shouted at his brother.

"Don't tell me you wouldn't have done the same," Hip said. "Let's just get this over with."

Therese got a better look at Jen and Hip and immediately realized what had happened. Hip had taken her place. Jen was a goddess. That was the only reason why she was still alive.

Therese didn't know what to feel, what to think.

"Get what over with?" Than asked.

"I'm taking her place," Hip said. "Take me to Charon."

"Let me take her and the twins to the Holts," Therese said. "She's still in danger here. She doesn't know how to fight."

Another lightning bolt zipped past.

"Hip, go with them," Than said. "Your soul isn't calling to me. Just go."

Therese led the way through the gates to Hades's chariot, where Swift and Sure hovered nervously between Pegasus on one side and Riptide, Seaquake, and Crest pulling Poseidon's chariot on the other. Cupid flew protectively near the animals with an arrow fitted, ready to strike.

Cupid helped them pile into the chariot. Hip took the reins in front with Jen beside him. Therese held the babies in the backseat. They flew away from the explosions and fire and sounds of thunder to the west, toward the San Juan Mountains.

Before they descended from the skies, Persephone appeared beside Therese in the backseat.

"Hypnos!" she cried. "Oh, my darling son! What have you done?"

Therese watched in silent anguish as the goddess tried to come to terms with the loss of her son's immortality.

"I love her, Mother," Hip said. "And she was going to die."

"I'm confused," Jen interrupted. "Are you talking about me?"

"He's given you his immortality," Persephone said, not with an accusatory tone, but not with kindness, either.

"Given it to me?" Jen looked to Therese for explanation.

"He made you a goddess," Therese said. "You would have died, otherwise."

Jen's mouth fell open. "But that means..." her voice dropped off as she sat on the bench in front of Therese beside Hip, in shock.

From the backseat, Persephone said, "It means he's no longer immortal. It means he'll die one day."

"Sooner than that," Hip said. "Than should be coming for me any moment."

"You're wrong," Persephone said. "You changed her before she died. Why would Thanatos come for you now?"

Hip's eyes widened as he turned back to look for confirmation from his mother. "That can't be."

"You will live as a mortal on earth in her place," Persephone said as tears rolled down her cheeks. "I suppose you can watch over Than and Therese's precious twins."

Therese felt the knot in her stomach tighten. She should be grateful, but instead, she was filled with envy.

"I gave Jen my immortality because I thought I'd go straight to the Elysian Fields. I can't go on without her."

The chariot descended into the familiar mountains behind Jen's house.

"Can't you take your immortality back?" Jen asked.

"The trade is irrevocable," Persephone cried. "What's done is done. Oh, Hip!"

The goddess flung her arms around her son and cried against his neck.

"This is so messed up," Jen said, breaking into tears. "I don't want to be a god without Hip."

Hip's eyes closed, and he slumped, sound asleep, into Jen's arms. Therese noticed the twins had also fallen into a deep sleep. The duties of sleep must have been transferred to Jen.

"What's happening to me?" Jen asked. "I'm being called in different directions all at once!"

Therese touched her hand and called for the duties of sleep to come to her. "Let me help you."

"Hades needs his chariot," Persephone said. "We must go at once."

"Take care of my babies for me," Therese said to Jen, handing them over. "Just until I can figure out what to do."

Persephone kissed each of her grandchildren. "They're so precious."

Therese felt herself disintegrating as restless mortals everywhere embraced sleep for the first time in weeks.

"What will I tell everyone?" Jen asked.

"I don't know."

"We have to go." Persephone carried her son from the chariot and laid him on the ground beneath a Cyprus tree.

"I'll return as soon as I can," Therese said, kissing the tops of her babies' heads.

As she and Persephone drove the chariot back to Mount Olympus and away from the newborn twins, another part of Therese died.

Chapter Twenty: Conundrums

Jen stood in the darkness behind her house holding Therese's babies with Hip asleep at her feet. Even though night had fallen, she could see clearly, as though the sun was bright in the sky. She also felt unencumbered by the two squirming infants. Although they were barely six pounds each, bouncing them around the grotto had given her a back ache over the past few days; tonight, they seemed light as a feather. She supposed what Therese had said was true: Jen was a goddess, and she was endowed with goddess strength.

She looked down at Hip, who yawned, stretched, and opened his eyes. She couldn't believe what he'd done for her. To save her life, he'd given up his immortality. Tears sprang to her eyes. His generosity and outpouring of love overwhelmed her.

As Hip blinked and looked up at her, it occurred to her that maybe their situation wasn't as bad as she had originally thought. They would have his entire lifetime together. That's really all she ever wanted: a lifetime together. She didn't care if he grew old. She would always love him and would take care of him up until the end.

And if it ever became too difficult for her to go on without him, maybe she could give her immortality away to someone else. Maybe she could give it to Bobby. She'd cross that bridge when she got to it. Right now, she was glad to be alive and glad to finally experience the depths of Hip's love for her.

Hip climbed to his feet and circled her waist with his arms.

"Are you okay?' he asked her.

She nodded. "Thank you."

He gave her a half smile. "I had no choice. I couldn't bear to go on…"

"You don't have to. We can still be together like this. I'll live down here, and when you die. I'll give my immortality to someone else."

Hip frowned as he cupped her face in both his hands. "We'll have each other in our dreams, like before."

It was Jen's turn to frown. "Why in our dreams. This isn't a dream."

"When I gave you my immortality, I also gave you my duties. You're the new goddess of sleep."

Jen felt her eyes grow wide with understanding. The excitement that had built up inside her chest deflated. "I don't get to decide what kind of goddess I want to be, like Therese did?"

Hip shook his head. "I'm sorry."

"I don't understand."

"I made a trade. It's hard to explain."

"Maybe I could be the goddess of animal companions and *she* could be the goddess of sleep. Then I could be with you."

"She can't do that, or she'll go mad. But she could take over for short periods, like she's doing right now."

"There has to be a way," she insisted.

He kissed her cheek and whispered, "Let's get the babies inside."

    ***

Therese flew through the night sky with Persephone in Hades's chariot, ready to help the other gods take back Mount Olympus. Disintegrated into the millions, she also helped bring rest back to humankind.

Thanatos met her at the gates and fought by her side, but elsewhere, he had resumed his duties as god of the dead, and he told her, where the Underworld and dream world met, that gathering the souls of Circe's undead army would be a job of cataclysmic proportions.

Before they parted at the very spot where she had first met Hypnos four years ago, he asked about the twins.

"They're with Hip and Jen," she said, trying not to cry.

She reminded herself that she would visit them often, and that this was the only way she could be a part of both her children and her husband's lives. Ares was wrong: she didn't have to choose. She couldn't be their mother, but she would be in their lives as often as possible.

She fitted one arrow after another to her bow and shot down zombies while avoiding blasts of lightning from the palace. At the same time, she sought out her twins and entered their dreams.

Not knowing if she'd ever have a chance to speak to them subconsciously again, she created a peaceful dream for each of them. She brought in figments to people their dreams with members from both Than's family and hers. She introduced them, pointing out their father and grandparents, and aunts and uncles.

This is Hades, and this is Persephone. And here are Carol and Richard. See these red birds? These, too—all of them—are your grandparents. And this is your Uncle Hip and your Aunt Lynn.

She showed them who they were named for. She wanted the babies to know how special they were, and how loved. She told them in the dream that they would one day restore faith to humanity.

So while one of her was destroying monster after monster in a whirlwind of chaos, blood, and fire, another of her was building dream after peaceful dream in a symphony of beauty, hope, and love.

***

Thanatos disintegrated into the hundreds and brought the Cyclopes to their knees. This enabled Hades, under the protection of the helm's power of invisibility, to get close enough to Circe to bind her, and for Poseidon to paralyze Menoetius with the trident. Zeus then took charge of the Cyclopes, and regained his power over them and the lightning bolts. Soon after, the black magic controlling the zombies was broken. The zombies fell to the ground, and their souls called to Thanatos.

The sheer numbers of dead were overwhelming. Never in his history had he been called by so many souls in a single day. What was worse, there were many who were past the time for calling and who were in danger of becoming lost forever. He sensed them as he was gathering others. He was about to ask his father about the problem when he ran into Melinoe in New York City, where the zombie population had been out of control.

Surprised to see her outside of Tartarus, he stared dumbly at her for a few moments where she was walking along 44th Street toward Time Square leading a parade of confused souls. She clicked her tongue, in a kind of cat call, and the souls flocked to her like ducklings. He watched for several seconds before she noticed him.

"Shocked, are you?" she said defensively.

"No, I…"

"Well, I'm just doing my job," she snapped. "Your father's orders."

"He asked you to do that?"

She rolled her eyes. "Don't worry. I'm bringing them to Charon."

He arched a brow, unsure whether he could believe her after so many centuries of enduring her sabotage.

She turned her back on him and resumed her clicking. He supposed he would have to trust her, and it was a credit to her that she'd been freed from Tartarus.

Back on Mount Olympus, the Olympians had finally ended the war and had captured their adversaries. It was decided that the court would convene in twenty-four hours to question the prisoners, determine their punishment, and delegate the duties of reparations. There was also the matter of the decision made by Hypnos to trade places with Jen Holt. All agreed to meet the following day.

Although Thanatos continued to guide the massive number of souls to Charon, he also met with Therese in their rooms, where they tried to comfort one another over the loss of their twins.

They sat together on their new couch facing the flames in the fireplace. Therese's legs were curled beneath her and her head lay against Than's chest. He stroked her red hair, as red as the flames of the Phlegethon. She traced her finger along his chest.

"We'll convince my father to allow us to switch duties from time to time," Than said. "While I'm Death, you can visit the children, and while you're Death, I'll visit them."

"But we'll never be together at the same time," Therese said.

"No."

"And they won't know who we are to them," she said. "They'll think of us as their aunt and uncle."

"But *we'll* know."

She lifted her tear-filled eyes to his. "I miss them so much. I can still feel them in my arms, their sweet little faces looking up at me. How long before I forget what that felt like?"

He had no words for her as tears brimmed in his own eyes.

"There are moments when I say to myself I can do this," she added. "But most of the time, I feel like I'm falling apart."

"I know." He stroked her hair and cupped her cheeks. "I miss them, too."

"What if I *can't* do this?" she asked him.

"What do you mean?"

"What if I end up like Dionysus because I just can't continue in my purpose?"

"You mean…"

"What if I go to earth and live with the twins and turn my back on my duties?"

"I don't think…"

"What about my duties to *them*?"

Than kissed her forehead and closed his eyes, afraid for what he was about to say next. It was an idea he'd been toying with, but it would break his heart if she decided to act on it.

"There is one way you could avoid the madness," he started.

Her face transformed from anguish to hope so quickly that his heart stopped beating.

"How?" she asked.

"You could give your immortality to Hip and take his place as a mortal." Than was suddenly nauseous at the thought of losing her.

Therese's face fell. "But then how would I be with *you*?"

Again, he had no words.

***

Hip took one of the babies from Jen and followed her toward the house. Indoor lights showed signs of people still awake in the Holt household, so as Jen opened the door and went inside, Hip wondered how she would explain.

Mrs. Holt and Mr. Stern looked up at them in surprise from the kitchen table where Mrs. Holt was sitting with the phone against one ear and a pen in her hand. She'd been scrawling on a notepad but had dropped the pen as soon as they had entered.

"She just walked in the door!" Mrs. Holt said into the phone. "Yes, officer, that's right. I'll call you back in the morning."

Mrs. Holt stood up, dropped the phone on the table, and gawked.

Mr. Stern stood as well, and Bobby, who'd been upstairs, came running down in his boxers and t-shirt.

Everyone stared at Hip and Jen in disbelief.

"Could you have called?" Mrs. Holt said as bewilderment turned to anger. "We've been worried sick."

"Calm down, Mom. It's not what you think," Jen said.

"I don't think anything, young lady," Mrs. Holt replied. "I don't know what to think."

"Can we sit down in the living room?" Jen asked. "And talk calmly like adults?"

Her mother looked from Hip to Jen and from one baby to the other. "Are those Therese's twins?"

"Can we please sit down?" Jen asked again. "You don't know what I've been through."

Hip followed Jen into the family room as Mrs. Holt said, "Alrighty, but you don't know what *I've* been through."

Jen's mother burst into tears.

Chapter Twenty-One: Aftermath

Thanatos stood in the great court beside Therese and his parents as Zeus and the others interrogated Circe and Menoetius. Circe ignored them in a cacophony of shrieks and cackles, punctuated with obscenities and, intermittently, "I don't care!" and "I couldn't care less!" and "Do what you will to me!" Menoetius, on the other hand, gave up everything. He and Atlas had hoped to subdue the gods and free the remaining Titans and had been using Circe to those ends. He promised that one day the Titans would reign again.

Atlas had already been returned to his post on the Atlas Mountains where he held Uranus on his shoulders and kept him from mating with Gaia.

It was decided that Menoetius would be returned to the pit of Tartarus where the other Titans were imprisoned, and Circe would join him. Than, his sisters, Hecate, and his parents would see to their internment.

Phorcys, Keto, Echidna, Chimera, Ladon, and Scylla were also brought in by Poseidon in his golden net. The monsters had all healed from their wounds with the return of their immortal strength, but as punishment for their collusion with Circe, they were confined to the ancient castle under house arrest indefinitely—except for Ladon, who would return to guarding Hera's golden apple tree.

Poseidon wanted them all thrown into the dungeon of Tartarus with the Titans, but he was out-voted. To appease him, the gods agreed that the monsters should be at Poseidon's beck and call, should he ever need them. The monsters were forced to swear on the River Styx to serve Poseidon and Amphitrite forever. Thoosa was included in that sentence, but seemed more than happy to serve.

It was determined that the Cyclopes who served Circe had been under an enchantment and so were not held responsible for their actions.

Ares, however, would stand trial in the following weeks for his part in freeing Atlas.

Then the duties of reparations were delegated, because all four realms—Olympus, Poseidon's palace, the Underworld, and the Upperworld—had sustained substantial damage.

Finally, the gods addressed the decision made by Hypnos to trade places with Jen Holt.

"Is there anything we can do to reverse the trade?" Persephone asked her colleagues.

Hades stepped forward and said, "I move that we call the Fates to court and question them on the matter."

Than was surprised by his father's motion. It made him wonder if there might be a chance to recover his brother's immortal status. Why else would his father call upon the Fates?

Five minutes later, his three great aunts appeared, wearing the same velvet suits he saw them in the last time he had visited, the time he and Therese had gone to ask how many children they would have. He and Therese had wanted to know so they could offer that number of golden apples to Ares and end his threat against them, but things hadn't worked out as they had hoped. The Fates had said he and Therese would have two children, but none immortal.

And, of course, they had been right.

"What a pleasant surprise," Lachesis, the measurer, and the plumpest of the three said as they entered from the rainbow steps. Her short curly hair appeared newly washed, and her blue velvet dress freshly pressed.

Clotho, the spinner, slapped her hand through the air, as though she were swatting a fly, and complained, "Oh, dearie. We knew we were coming eventually. We just couldn't see when."

She adjusted the jacket of her pink velvet pantsuit as she moved toward the center of the court. Some of her gray hair was piled in a bun on top of her head, and the rest of it fell down her back.

Atropos, the cutter, removed her lavender jacket, primped her bob with one hand, and said, "It's warm up here."

"Welcome to Mount Olympus," Zeus said.

Hera said, "Iris, please bring them some refreshments."

Hera's messenger goddess obeyed by flying across the hall to the dining room. Hestia excused herself and followed.

"How about a cigarette?" Clotho asked.

"It's too bad we don't get invited to places more often," Lachesis said. "What a thrill when Hermes first appeared."

"I thought you preferred isolation," Hades said.

"Oh, we do." Clotho flapped her hand once again through the air. "It's just the invitation we enjoy. That's the only part we can't see."

Than recalled what the Fates had once told him: The threads of gods are woven, but they are neither measured nor cut like they are for the mortals. The threads belonging to the Fates remain unwoven, for the sake of their sanity. They don't know the details of their own futures, except when they cross paths with another.

"We'll be sure to remember that," Persephone said with a smile.

"We won't come, you know," Clotho said. "We just like being invited."

"Why won't you come?" Aphrodite asked.

"Because they're accosted by those wanting to see their futures," Apollo said. "I get that a lot, too."

"Absolutely," Atropos replied. "And it never ends well."

Iris and Hestia returned with a small table full of pomegranates and ambrosia. Hermes snapped his fingers to conjure them each a chair and a cigarette.

"We've asked you here today to discuss trades," Hades said. "Specifically the one recently made by Hypnos."

269

"Oh," Lachesis said, drawing out the syllable so that it resembled the moo of a cow.

"Oh, yes," Atropos said, as she exhaled her cigarette smoke. "I see where we are now."

"Oh, poo," Clotho complained. "I was just beginning to enjoy myself, too."

"Our apologies, dear aunts," Persephone said. "But this is of grave importance to us."

"It's always of grave importance to everyone we meet." Atropos sighed, with great exaggeration, it seemed to Than.

Demeter lifted her brows, apparently offended.

"We need to know if Hypnos can take back his immortality," Zeus clarified.

"Yes," Lachesis said. "Yes, he can."

Than noticed the faces of nearly everyone in the room become brighter, especially his mother's.

"That's wonderful!" Persephone cried.

"Indeed!" Athena exclaimed.

"The mortal girl will die, of course," Clotho pointed out before taking another draft from her cigarette.

"Immediately," Atropos added.

Than glanced at Therese, whose face had gone pale.

"If that's true," Aphrodite said, "then I don't think Hip will take his immortality back. His love for her is too strong."

"Of course it's true," Clotho barked.

"We don't lie," Lachesis said, more kindly.

"That's not what I meant." Aphrodite rushed across the room and laid her hands on the shoulders of Clotho and Lachesis. "I didn't mean to offend you." Then she waved her hand in front of her face to clear away the cigarette smoke hovering in the center of the court. "I should have said, 'in that case.'"

"So we're back to square one," Artemis said.

Rhea cleared her throat and lifted a manly finger. "Unless someone else is willing to take Hypnos's place. Isn't that so, Atropos?"

"Absolutely," the cutter replied.

Than suspected he wasn't the only god to think of the possibility of Therese making the offer to trade with his brother. He reached over and held her hand. He could feel her looking at him, but he could not return her gaze. He wanted his brother back, but he didn't want to lose his wife.

I should do this, she prayed to him. *I should be the one to make the trade. It's the only thing that makes sense.*

He couldn't look at her. He didn't want her to see the agony that had taken possession of his features, the tears that were threatening to well up in his eyes. He cleared his suddenly tight throat and swallowed hard before replying. *Only you can make that decision.*

   ***

Therese closed her eyes and imagined her babies' faces as she clutched her lockets. Each hour that passed since she had last held them in her arms made it more and more difficult for her to imagine them. Only when Jen lifted up a prayer to her, was she able to see a glimpse of her precious twins through Jen's eyes.

She needed to be with them.

Thanatos squeezed her hand as they listened to the gods question the Fates, and she squeezed it back. She tried to study his face, to get a sense of what he thought she should do, but he wouldn't look at her. He didn't want to affect her decision.

But she wanted to know what he hoped she would do. Did he want her to stay with him and allow their babies to be raised by someone else? Or did he think she should go, with the hope that they would be able to visit one another regularly?

Only you can make that decision, came his reply.

Before she had given birth, she believed she would ask her aunt and uncle to raise the babies, and if they said no, she would ask Jen.

But once she gave birth and held her babies in her arms, the idea of leaving them to be raised by others made her sick to her stomach. Her maternal instinct was overwhelming. It wasn't that she didn't trust her aunt and uncle, or Jen and Hip, to raise them properly. She knew either couple would give the twins ample love and good lives; but she wanted to be their mother. She wanted to be with them each day. She didn't want to see them grow from afar; she wanted to be right there, teaching them how to take their first steps, in everything they did. And, if she were to be honest with herself, she would have to admit she wanted to age with them.

Maybe it was because she was born a mortal, but whatever the reason, she clung to a romantic vision of growing old with Thanatos and their children. She still dreamed of having grandchildren, of sitting in a rocking chair beside Than on their front porch looking out at the mountains of Colorado, while their grandchildren played in the grass near their feet, sipping lemonade and eating homemade cookies.

She could have this dream if she traded with Hip—all of it except for the part of having Thanatos by her side. She would age, but he would always look like a boy of eighteen.

When she imagined him coming to her for visits—she an old woman and he a young man, she shuddered.

Than must have felt her shudder, for he looked at her at that moment, and it allowed her to see the agony and concern on his face. He was as torn as she over what she should do.

A memory of her father helping her make a decision when she was thirteen flashed through her mind. He had helped her to decide between band camp and an out-of-town swim meet. If she competed in the meet, she would miss the whole week of camp, and there were plenty of meets and only one camp a year; but she was in the first heat against Lacey Holzmann, who had just beaten her in their most recent competition.

Her father had told her to close her eyes and to imagine what the entire week would be like if she were to choose the swim meet. After five minutes, he asked her what she saw. She described in minute detail how she had beat Lacey. Then her father asked her to close her eyes and imagine what the entire week would be like if she were to choose band camp. After five minutes, as before, he asked her what she saw. She said the whole time she was at camp, she was wondering if she would have beat Lacey.

"Then you have your answer," he had said.

So Therese closed her eyes and imagined her life with her babies in Colorado. She saw herself teaching them to walk, to swim, to ride horses. She saw herself teaching them to feed the chipmunks and the wild horses. She saw herself on her aunt and uncle's deck with a pair of binoculars to her face, and she was pointing out the wildlife in the mountains across the Lemon Reservoir to her children, just as she used to do with her father. As the gods continued to discuss options for Hip, her mind went wild with excitement.

Then she opened her eyes and closed them again, this time imagining a life with Thanatos. She imagined being beside him, loving him, holding him, but these images were soon overpowered, and all she could see was an eternity of wondering what a life with her children might have been like.

She knew her answer.

"I'll take his place," Therese said to the court. "I will give my immortality to Hypnos."

*****

Jen loaded the groceries into her pick up and then headed back home. This was the first time in her life that she'd pulled an all-nighter and hadn't felt tired. She could also carry a ton of bags in her arms and get everything indoors in one trip. It didn't matter that the sun hadn't completely made its appearance, because she could see in the dark. Being a goddess had its perks.

She was looking forward, for instance, to learning how to fly and to god travel. As sad as she was that Hip was now a regular human being (which, let's face it, was not such a bad thing—just about everyone she knew was one), she couldn't quell the excitement over her new super powers. It hadn't really sunk in that she wouldn't be seeing him or her family on a regular basis.

The babies were crying and ready to eat as soon as Jen arrived home, so she took Hestia from her mother while her mother mixed the formula. Jen tore open the packages of diapers and wipes she had bought and got to work cleaning each baby with Hip's help. Unlike her, Hip was tired and not ready to be awake. She sent him back to bed as soon as her mother had the bottles made. Jen and her mom sat together on the couch in the early dawn and fed the babies.

"I want you to know right now, Mom," Jen started. "I am never having kids."

"I guess I'll have to depend on Bobby to give me grandchildren, then."

"Good luck with that."

"I still can't believe how Hip saved your life," her mom said. "He gave up so much for you."

Jen nodded as she adjusted the burp cloth beneath little Hermes's chin.

"He must really love you," her mother added.

"We want to be married," Jen said.

Her mother frowned.

Jen bent her brows and asked, "Aren't you happy for me?"

"Do you think that's fair to him?" Mrs. Holt asked. "You said you won't get to visit us often, except in our dreams. What kind of marriage will that be? And you don't want to give him children to keep him company."

It was Jen's turn to frown. "Not everything can be perfect all the time."

"Nothing's ever perfect," Mrs. Holt said. "But this sounds like a really bad deal for poor Hip. He'll be alone most of his life after giving up so much for you."

"So you want me to dump him?"

"No, of course not. But maybe don't marry him. Give him the chance to move on later, if he so desires."

This idea just about broke Jen's heart.

"I'm sorry, baby doll. I'll mind my own business."

"Good idea," Jen said, but inside, she was considering her mother's words. Would Jen be hurting Hip by marrying him?

"So, new subject. When are we going to tell Carol and Richard about these babies?"

Hermes spit the bottle out, so Jen moved him to her shoulder and patted his back to burp him.

"We have to wait for Therese," Jen said. "She'll tell us what to do."

"When?"

"I don't know." Then Jen asked, "What if her aunt and uncle say no? What if they don't want the twins?"

Her mother sighed. "Try not to worry, baby girl. We'll figure out something."

***

Hip was glad to be out of the house and outside, even though it meant hard work, and he didn't have his godly strength to help him. Brushing Hershey beat feeding babies and changing diapers any day, even if those babies were his cute little niece and nephew.

Bobby and Jen were fun to hang out with, too, and Mrs. Holt didn't seem to mind staying inside and taking care of the babies. Mr. Stern was inside helping her.

"By the way," Jen said as she returned her brush to a shelf in the barn. "Do you have any more dream globes?"

"Sorry," Hip said. "Yours is the only one. Why?"

"What's a dream globe?" Bobby asked.

"Oh, no."

"What's wrong?" Hip moved closer to her.

"I kind of destroyed it when I saw you with Pashitia."

"Who's Pashitia?" Bobby asked.

"You destroyed my Christmas present?"

"You were with the evil lord of the Sith!"

"Well, it was a one-of-a-kind gift from the Fates. It would have been nice to have over the years, to get in touch with you."

Jen frowned.

"I guess I'm invisible," Bobby said. "Maybe I got super powers, too."

"Hold on," Hip said, suddenly feeling funny.

As he looked down at the hay, a tingle ran from the top of his head to the tips of his fingers and toes. He immediately recognized what was happening, but he was completely bewildered. How was his immortality coming back to him?

A thud brought him from his reverie.

"Bobby?" Jen ran to her brother's side. He'd fallen on the ground. "He won't wake up. The horses are asleep now, too. Did the duties of sleep come back to me?"

"Not to you," Hip said, incredulous. "To me."

Chapter Twenty-Two: Goodbyes

Therese tried not to shiver from the cold as she followed Than to her favorite bat cave. The light from the Phlegethon was dim here, and she could barely see. She was also unused to not having her bow and quiver slung around her shoulder, but there was no need to carry them now.

"I'm going to miss this place," she said.

"Hades promised to let you and the twins visit," he reminded her.

"He and Persephone just want to see their grandbabies," Therese said. "I doubt he'll allow me to roam around for nostalgia's sake."

"He might."

Therese smiled at the image of their twins running around in her bat cave and playing with the rats and mice. She imagined them throwing rocks into the Phlegethon, feeding cakes to Cerberus and Hydra, and rocking Charon's boat. Oh, how fun it will be to bring them here, she thought. She only hoped Hades would allow it often.

She had a feeling he just might.

Allowing her and the twins to visit wasn't the only promise Hades had made: he had also promised to restore Melinoe to an honorable position among the gods of the Underworld. Her job was to collect the souls who, for whatever reason, failed to call to Than, usually because they'd been distracted by a malevolent being. Although she didn't have the power of disintegration, Melinoe did have the ability to collect multiple souls at a time, and she would then lead them all to Charon.

Hades had also promised that, as a reward for her sacrifice during the battle with Atlas, Melinoe would be given one night a year to go back to her old ways of frightening mortals with an entourage of ghosts. Whatever souls she collected on that one day would join her in her antics before being escorted to Charon and their judgment. Melinoe was allowed to choose the night, and she quickly settled on her favorite time of the year.

Halloween.

Along with those promises, it was decided in court while the Fates were present that all souls, no matter the crime, should have a chance at redemption. Therese hadn't made this a condition of her trade with Hip, but she had asked for it on the heels of her offer, and all the gods were so grateful to her for taking Hip's place, that they worked together to find a loophole in the ancient law. Therese had realized then that, although most of them had come to love her, they couldn't help but love Hypnos more.

Despite all these promises, Hades hadn't been able to help Than. Before they'd left the court, Than had asked if it was possible for Jen to remain the god of sleep and for Hip to take over as the god of death so that Than could become a mortal with Therese.

Hope had flared inside of Therese's chest until the Fates said that immortality had to be traded, not renounced.

"You will go mad," Clotho had said. "Even as a mortal."

"You have to trade fates with another," Atropos had explained.

"Everything has to be balanced," Lachesis had added.

Persephone had laid a hand on Than's shoulder and had said, "Don't do this, please. You'll break my heart."

"It's basically a death sentence," Hades had said. "If you trade with someone, you won't know that person's fate. You could get hit by a bus and die that very day."

"And what good would you be to Therese or your twins then?" Demeter had asked.

Than had said he couldn't bestow the burden on someone else, anyway—not without that person's consent.

"I would need to know the mortal is willing," Than had said.

"No one wants to be Death," Zeus had said. "So that settles the matter."

Therese had understood, but she had also died a little more.

Than reached the cave and turned to face her. "You okay?"

She nodded, but she was breathing heavily. The hike was a lot harder without her godly strength and endurance.

He took her hands. "What did Clifford decide?"

"He has no choice. He's coming with me." Besides, he wanted to come with her. He could return to Than later, after Therese…she didn't want to think about that.

"And Jewels?"

"Also with me, but I'm leaving Stormy here for Jen. A familiar face will comfort her."

"Is there any place else we need to see before we go?"

She had already been to Tartarus to say goodbye to Pete, Tiresias, and the Furies. Pete had turned down his chance to move on to the Elysian Fields, because he wanted to be with Tizzie, but Tiresias wanted to go. When he was ready, she'd accompanied him, because she wanted to say goodbye to Vicki, even though Vicki no longer recognized her. After that, Therese had some time with Cubie and Galin. Hecate and Persephone had said their goodbyes to her on Mount Olympus along with the others.

It was difficult to say goodbye to all the gods on Mount Olympus, because unlike the gods of the Underworld, Therese would likely never see them again. They made promises to visit her, but she didn't expect those promises to be kept. She knew they were all busy with their duties, and also that the passing of time for the gods was unlike that for mortals.

"Are you ready then?" Than asked.

He must be anxious to see the babies, she thought—as anxious as she was. "I guess so."

She said goodbye to the bats, even though she could no longer hear their replies. Then she sent up a prayer of thanks to Hecate, who had taken over the duties of death so Than could drive her home. She followed Than through the cold winding tunnels from the bat cave to the stables, where Clifford and Jewels were already waiting for her in the chariot.

　　　***

Than stole glances at Therese as they flew across the afternoon sky toward Colorado. Helios was in his cup at high noon, but Than doubted Therese could recognize him as anything but an orb of light. She waved at the sun god anyway, and this brought a smile to Than's lips.

He parked the chariot in the woods behind the Holts' place. Clifford jumped out, excited to be home. He headed directly for the stream, where he loved to chase the trout. Jewels climbed out, too, and followed, which surprised Therese and made her laugh.

Than loved to see her laugh.

Although it was not yet autumn, when his mother would return to the Underworld from Mount Olympus, it was late enough in September for the trail rides to have ended, so none of the Holts were outside or in the barn as Than and Therese hiked their way to the back door.

Hip opened the door before they knocked. Apparently, he'd been waiting for them. Jen was by his side.

"I can't thank you enough," he said to Therese.

"Me either!" Jen cried. "Are you okay?"

"I'm fine. How are the twins?" she asked, yawning.

"Sound asleep," Hip replied. "The whole house is asleep."

"Now I know to call on *you* when I can't get the babies down," Therese said with a smile. Then she added, "It's good to see you back to normal," just before she collapsed into Than's arms.

"I better go," Hip said. "I'll catch you later, bro'." Hip turned to Jen. "You're okay riding back with Than?"

Jen nodded. "See you soon."

Hip leaned in for a kiss from Jen.

As soon as Hip had disappeared, Than was able to arouse Therese from her sleep. At the same time, the rest of the house began waking up, including the babies.

Than and Therese found them on pallets on the living room floor beside Mrs. Holt and Mr. Stern, who had fallen asleep on the rug beside them. Bobby was stretching and opening his eyes from where he lay on the couch.

Mr. Stern and Mrs. Holt sat up just as Than and Therese each picked up a twin.

"Well, hello there," Mrs. Holt said with surprise.

Than forgot to reply. He was too mesmerized by Hestia and Hermes. Mr. Stern and Mrs. Holt must have realized this, for they left the room, calling for Bobby and Jen to follow.

"I need to feed them," Therese said to Than, as she sat down on the couch. "Will you help me?"

"With pleasure."

He moved beside her and cradled Hestia as Therese fed Hermes. He gazed at Hestia, trying to memorize the features of her face, even though he knew they would change daily. When Hermes had had enough of Therese's milk, Than traded babies and burped Hermes. Then he gazed at his little face, too.

They sat together for a little more than an hour before they left the Holts' and made their way over to Therese's childhood home, hoping Carol and Richard would be willing to take her and the babies in.

    ***

"We'll tell them we adopted," Therese told Than as they walked up the dirt road to her old house, each with a baby. "It's only been two months since they last saw me, and I did *not look* seven months pregnant then."

"You sure you don't want to tell them the truth?" Than asked. "I'll sound like such a douche bag, having to stay away from my family because of my work."

"That's not exactly a lie," Therese said.

"That I'm a douche bag?" he asked.

"No, silly!" She laughed. "That you have to stay away because of your work."

"I'd like for them to understand that I don't have a choice," he said.

"Maybe I can tell them some day. I'm worried it will frighten them."

"Mrs. Holt and Bobby seem to be handling it without any problems," he argued.

"But Hip and Jen aren't *Death*," Therese said. "I'm worried they'll be freaked out by the idea that I'm married to *Death*."

"Oh."

Now Therese felt like the douche bag. "Plus, I'm worried they'll treat the babies differently."

"I suppose you know them better than I do."

When they reached the gravelly drive leading up to the house, Therese's mom and dad flew over to greet them.

For the first time since making her offer to trade with Hip, Therese realized one more price she'd have to pay: she couldn't communicate with her parents. Their songs sounded like those of any other cardinals.

Tears filled her eyes.

"I can't understand them anymore," she said to Than.

He put a comforting arm around her waist as the red birds came and landed on each of the blankets swaddling the twins.

"I'll explain everything to them," Than said.

"Do you think they can still understand *me*?" she asked.

"I know they can."

She sighed with relief as she batted tears away with her one free hand.

"Hi, Mom and Dad," she said to them.

They tweeted back.

"Therese!" Carol swung open the door of the screened-in front porch and called out to her and Than.

Therese's parents flew back to their elm tree.

Lynn ran up and hugged Therese's legs before she had made it through the door.

"Terry!" Lynn said in her sweet little voice. "You have babies?"

"Let's go inside and sit down," Therese said. "I need to talk to Mama and Daddy."

"Mama and Daddy" were the names Lynn had given Carol and Richard, so Therese used them when she was talking to Lynn.

"Daddy's not home. Can you talk to me?" Lynn asked with a hopeful smile.

"Of course!" Therese said.

Lynn reached up her arms to Than to be picked up, so Than used his free arm to scoop her up on his hip.

"What's baby's name?" Lynn asked, as they made their way to the living room couch.

"This is Hermes," Than replied. "And that's Hestia."

"Are they your babies?" Lynn asked Than.

Therese's heart melted as she watched Than's face break into the sweetest smile. "Yes, they are. Mine and Terry's."

"So tell me what's going on," Carol said as she sat across from them in Richard's recliner.

"These babies were in need of a home, so we decided to adopt," Therese lied.

"Wow," Carol said, apparently in shock. "So the adoption has already been finalized?"

Therese nodded. "I guess this makes you and Richard grandparents, sort of."

"I guess it does."

"Aren't you happy for us?" Therese asked, feeling the blood rush to her face.

"Of course, but I can't believe I am just now hearing about this. I would have asked if you were sure you were ready, but I guess now it's too late."

"I'm sorry." Therese knew there was no way around a litany of apologies.

"And I would have thrown you a shower," Carol added. "Maybe I still can."

"Don't go to any trouble," Than said, though Therese arched a brow his way. She wanted a shower.

"Are Than's parents able to help you?"

Therese cleared her throat. "Sort of, but…"

"That's why we're here," Than broke in. "Therese and I think it would be better for the babies if they were raised up here…in Colorado."

"You're moving here?" Carol jumped from her chair and leaned over to hug each of them. "Can I hold one of them?"

Therese handed her Hestia.

"Oh my gosh, she has red hair!" Carol said. "And she actually looks a little like you. How lucky!"

Therese felt another blush coming on as she and Than exchanged smiles.

"This is really interesting," Carol said, bouncing Hestia in her arms. "Because you won't believe where Richard is right now."

"Where?" Than and Therese asked simultaneously.

"He's closing on the purchase of the Melner Cabin."

"What? Why?" Therese asked.

"We were tired of all the strangers that come and go over there, especially now that Lynn is getting around more outdoors. So we made the Melners an offer, and after some going back and forth, they accepted."

"What are you planning to do with it?" Than asked.

"We *were* planning on finding a long-term renter," Carol said. "But I'm sure Richard would agree that you would make us the happiest grandparents in the world if you would move in!"

Therese frowned. "Well, the thing is…"

Than interrupted her. "It sounds like too good a deal to pass up."

"Wonderful!" Carol said. "I'm calling Richard right now to tell him the good news!"

Carol went to the phone in the kitchen to make her call.

Therese turned to Than and muttered, "What are you doing? I don't want to live alone with the twins in the Melner Cabin."

"I'm not giving up," he whispered. "Somehow, some way, I'll make our dream happen."

Therese studied his face and noticed he had the same expression he had worn four years ago, when she had failed to kill McAdams and he had promised to come back for her.

She filled with hope.

Carol hung up the phone and returned to the family room. "It's all settled."

"I just need to go home and take care of a few loose ends first," Than said to Carol. "Can Therese and the twins stay with you until I return?"

"Of course!" Carol said. "I'd love that!"

***

Hypnos was having a hard time teaching Jen to fly.

"Why can't you just trust me?" he asked her from the tip of Mount Ida, where he had introduced Jen to Asterion and Ariadne.

Dionysus was off dancing and drinking with the Maenads and Curetes at the bottom of the mountain and had no interest in night Frisbee.

"Just give her time," Ariadne said. "It takes practice."

"I'm scared to death," Jen said. "It's not natural to me. Put me on a horse, and I'm fine, but just free-floating in the wind? That's creepy."

Hip threw his hands in the air. "But it's hard to play night Frisbee on Stormy's back."

"And harder still if she won't fly," Asterion pointed out.

"Can we please just god travel back and get Stormy?" Jen asked.

Hip took her hand. "Fine, but if you don't practice, you'll never master it, just like with the bow and arrow."

"I don't like the bow and arrow," Jen said. "And I'm not the goddess of animal companions, okay?"

"Then what are you the goddess of?" Hip asked.

"I don't know yet. But not that."

Hip groaned. She'd better figure it out soon. If she didn't within three months, she'd lose her immortality and Therese's sacrifice will have been for nothing.

He'd never known anyone who could make him so angry and so happy all within five minutes.

Before they god traveled away, Than appeared.

"Hey, bro'!" Hip clapped a hand on Than's shoulder. "God, am I glad to see you."

"I need your help," Than said solemnly.

"Anything. Name it," Hip said, as the other three gathered around Than on the mountain top.

"Is there something we can do?" Asterion asked.

"Maybe." Than glanced at each of them with a determined look on his face. "I need ideas. There has to be a way for me to live a mortal life with the rest of my family without renouncing my immortality and going mad, or choosing some random mortal to make a trade."

"You want to die?" Ariadne asked. Then she murmured, "Death wants to die. How strange."

"You don't get it," Than said. "I don't want to die; I want to live. Before I met Therese four years ago, I wasn't really living. I was going through the motions, but I wasn't *alive*. My life began when I met her. Without her and the twins, my life is over. I'll go back to feeling like a puppet, like Sisyphus and his rock."

He looked at Hip and added, "This isn't about choosing death. It's about choosing life. Understand?"

Hip *did* understand.

"That's freakin' beautiful," Jen said.

"All my life, I've accepted things without question," Than said. "I've done my duty with few complaints."

"Ain't that the truth," Hip said.

"Well, I've changed. I want to shape my own destiny."

"We're here for you, Than," Asterion said.

292

"Maybe we could ask Pete," Jen said. "If we find a mortal willing to give him some blood…"

"Wait!" Hip snapped his fingers. "That's it!"

"What are you talking about?" Asterion asked.

Hip took Jen by the shoulders and gave her a quick peck on the mouth. "You're a genius!"

"Will you just spill the beans?" Ariadne demanded.

"Pete saw himself as the god of death," Hip replied.

"That makes no sense," Than said. "He has no corporeal body. He can't become a god."

"No sense," Jen said. "That's exactly what he muttered over and over again."

"Maybe Apollo knows," Hip said. "Someone must. If Pete saw it…"

"The visions of seers aren't as reliable as those of the Fates," Than reminded him.

Hip squeezed his brother's shoulder. "Isn't it worth checking out?"

Chapter Twenty-Three: The Gatekeeper's Promise

Jen rode on Stormy's back across the morning sky toward Colorado. Hip flew beside her, still worried she didn't know what she was doing.

"I'm telling you, I got this," she told him.

"What if I just want to be with you?" He winked.

She grinned. "You liar."

Flying was much less scary to Jen with a horse beneath her. In fact, seeing her house from up here, with the sun sparkling on the reservoir, the tree-tops on the mountain peaks already dusted with snow—well, it was downright magnificent.

"Where are you going first?" he asked her.

"Therese's." She began to descend toward the San Juan Mountains behind Carol and Richard's house. "I'm saving my visit with Mom for last. We have a lot to talk about before the wedding."

"Oh, boy. Better you than me."

Jen laughed.

"I better go before I put the whole area to sleep."

"See you tonight."

Hip disappeared, leaving Jen to land Stormy on her own. Luckily, Stormy knew exactly what to do.

"I'll be back in a bit," she told the horse as she dismounted and headed for Therese's back door.

Carol and Richard greeted Jen and congratulated her on her engagement. Lynn ran up to be held, so Jen picked her up and then carried her over to the couch to sit beside Therese.

"Hey, Jen." Therese smiled up at her.

"Do you always have a baby in your arms?" Jen asked.

Therese laughed. "It's hard to avoid with twins. I can't get them on the same sleeping schedule."

"That's *my* baby," Lynn said.

"Come out on the deck with us, Lynn," Richard called. "We want to show you something."

"Deer?" Lynn asked.

"Yep. And chipmunks," Carol said.

Lynn scurried across the room to her parents, giving Jen and Therese some privacy.

"Do you have news for me?" Therese asked.

Jen held out her arms for Hermes. "Can I hold him?"

Therese passed the little guy over.

"He's gotten so big."

"A lot has happened here in two weeks," Therese said. "They can hold up their heads on their own and sleep for four hours at a time."

"Yay for you, Hermes!" Jen said in a high-pitched voice. Then she turned to Therese. "Well, not much has happened for Than yet, but he's not giving up."

Therese frowned.

"He's meeting with Hades today, though," Jen added. "And Hip thinks they may have found a way."

"I hope so."

Hestia began fussing from her pallet on the floor, so Therese picked her up and began to nurse her.

"I came here to tell you something else," Jen said.

"Okay?"

"Promise not to be mad."

"Oh, no. What."

"Promise?"

"How can I promise if I don't know what it is?"

"I can't be the goddess of animal companions," Jen said. "It's just not who I am. I mean, I love animals, but not as much as you do—except for horses, of course."

"So, have you figured out your purpose?"

"Oh, good. You're not mad."

"I totally get it, Jen. Really." Therese added, "It was *my* purpose, not yours. And it still is. I'm going to open my own shelter here in a few years, when the twins are older."

"That's a great idea."

Therese smiled. "So what are you going to do, then?"

"Well, I have figured it out. And, boy, is Hip relieved. I couldn't get him off my back."

"So? What is it?"

"I'm the goddess of abused children," Jen said, with her chin held high. "I know how to help because I know how it feels."

Jen was surprised to see tears spring to Therese's eyes. "I'm so happy for you, Jen. I really am. I think that's just great."

Jen smiled. "Thanks. I do, too."

***

Thanatos sat across from his mother and father in their chambers.

"What is this about?" Than asked, suspiciously. "There's nothing you can say to change my mind. I love both of you, but I want to be with my wife and children, and I will keep searching until I find a way."

Persephone reached over and squeezed Hades's hand.

"There's something I have to tell both of you," Hades said.

Persephone's eyebrows furled and her lips parted. "What is it? You sound so somber."

"The Fates asked me to make a promise to them a few months ago, and I have just been told today to share it with you."

Than's heartbeat increased as he took a deep breath. "I'm listening."

"I was asked to swear on the River Styx not to say anything about the matter until they notified me. I had no idea what it all meant and was told my interference would ruin the lives of my children. So I said nothing."

Persephone sat on the edge of her chair. "You're frightening me."

"I'm sorry, Dear," Hades said, patting her hand. "This news will not sit well with you, I'm afraid."

"Please, Father," Than said impatiently. "Tell us what it is."

"When Peter Holt was struck down by Hermes's spear on your wedding day," Hades began, "the Fates ordered me to preserve the body."

Than's mouth fell open. The wheels turned quickly in his head. He dared not get his hopes up as he waited for his father to finish.

"Although they gave no explanation at the time, today they told me it was time to tell Thanatos. They said Pete had a special destiny and that you would know what to do."

Thanatos jumped from his chair and was about to shout a hooray when his mother's tears held him in check.

He bent close to her and kissed her cheek. She reached up, wrapped her arms around him, and wept.

The appearance of Tizzie a few moments later gave him the occasion to stand up and break from his mother's embrace. As he listened to Hades's explanation to his sister, Than noticed a smile of understanding creep across the Fury's face.

Tizzie turned to Than. "Shall we ask him together?"

Than returned her smile, and, together, they went to Tartarus to the seers' pit.

***

When Therese saw the bright yellow monster truck rolling down the dirt road toward Jen's house, she picked up the skirt of her bridesmaid's dress and ran out to greet it.

All decked out in their matching gray tuxedos, Ray and Todd climbed down and gave her a hug.

"It's been forever!" she said.

"Tell us about it," Ray laughed.

"We thought about taking a road trip to Texas just to see you," Todd added as he lifted his arm up to the driver's side to help out another passenger.

"Who's that?" Therese asked Ray.

"His date."

Therese's jaw nearly hit the floor when Gina Rizzo climbed out. Her golden curls were swooped up in a bun and her bright green dress looked beautiful on her.

"Hello, Therese," Gina said.

"Hi, Gina."

"So you're a mom now," Ray said, apparently trying to divert the tension. "Congratulations."

"Twins," she said. "Can you believe it?"

"No," Gina said. "You look too good to have just had twins."

299

"Well, we adopted," Therese lied.

"Even so, you look great," Gina said.

"Thanks." Then she added. "Come and meet them. My in-laws are holding them."

Therese giggled at the idea of introducing her friends to Hades and Persephone, lord and lady of the Underworld.

Most of the wedding guests had yet to arrive. Ray and Todd had come early because Jen and Mrs. Holt had asked them to be ushers again. Gina hung out with Therese until it was time for Therese to join the wedding party inside the house.

Thanatos looked so hot in his tux, that Therese didn't think she could wait for the wedding to end and to be home at the Melner Cabin. She distracted herself by puffing out Lynn's flower girl dress and reminding her to smile at all the guests.

Mrs. Holt looked absolutely beautiful in her cream-colored wedding gown, but Jen stole the show in her white sweetheart bodice and long, flowing train. Bobby stood between them with one on each arm, for it was his job to give them away.

Thanatos came by for a quick kiss before following Hip and Mr. Stern outside to wait for the procession. As Therese took her turn to walk down the aisle behind Lynn, she noticed her parents circle around a nearby Cypress tree and settle in its branches to watch. She winked at them and continued down to the front of the ceremony. She waved at Carol and Richard as she passed them. Halfway there, Than took her arm and escorted her to her spot before joining Hip at his side. Hip stood between

Than and Mr. Stern, looking happy if not a little nervous. It was a great day for a double wedding.

Therese's heart melted at the sight of Hades and Persephone sitting in the front row of the groom's side, with little Hermes and Hestia in their laps. Many of the other gods were there, too, including the beautiful Aphrodite and her Graces, accompanied by Ares and Hephaestus. Zeus and Hera, Apollo and Artemis, Hermes and Hecate, and Meg and Alecto were also there. Pete and Tizzie, newlyweds, had stayed behind so as not to horrify the mortals with evidence of Pete's resurrection, but they had sent their best wishes.

As Therese gazed out at her wonderful family and friends and then met Than's eyes across the aisle, she fought back tears of joy.

But when Jen reached over to hand Therese the bouquet before joining hands with Hip for the vows, Jen whispered, "Hip and I will have to leave right after the ceremony."

"Why?" Therese asked.

"Apparently Scylla and Charybdis have instigated a fight with Rhode, and Poseidon is up in arms over it," Jen whispered. "All the gods will have to go. Except for Ares, of course. He can't go until he finishes serving his sentence."

Jen was talking about the decision made by the other gods to sentence Ares to one year of barn duty for the soon-to-be Mr. and Mrs. Stern, which the gods saw as decent compensation for all of the turmoil the gods had caused the Holt family in recent years.

"We'll leave right after we cut the cake," Jen added.

Therese stifled a smile. Jen had some exciting adventures ahead of her, but Therese was happy with the one awaiting her right here in Colorado.

A Note from the Author

As many of you may know, this saga was originally intended to be a trilogy; but, when readers asked for more, I was more than happy to keep writing about these characters. I love them as much as, if not more than, you do. And I love this ending for Thanatos and Therese. After all, what more could any of us want than a long, happy life on earth with children destined for greatness?

But many of you disagree. You want more for Than and Therese. You want them to have a chance to regain their immortality. And you want their adventures to continue. You also want to know more about Hip and Jen and their lives together in the Underworld.

So I created another series called *A Gatekeeper's Spin-Off*. I decided against writing a seventh *Gatekeeper's Saga* book so that readers who want to quit after six books have that option. But now readers who want to continue can go on with the spin-off series, beginning with *Hypnos*, which released in November 2016.

The second book in the spin-off is *Hunting Prometheus*, which released in May 2017. The third and final book, *Storming Olympus,* released in May of 2018.

I also wrote a prequel to *The Gatekeeper's Saga* called *The Gatekeeper's Bride*. It can be read before or after the rest of the series. It released in April 2016. Another stand-alone that shares the world of The Gatekeeper's Saga is my novel,

Charon's Quest. It can be read at any time with the rest of the series.

Thank you for making this series a bestseller.

To find out more about me and my books, please visit my website at http://www.evapohler.com.

CPSIA information can be obtained
at www.ICGtesting.com
Printed in the USA
LVHW080227170819
628029LV00026B/1063/P